THE APPLAUSE WAS EDITED OUT!

Stephen Hudson

Publisher's Disclaimer

This is a work of fiction. All names, characters, places, businesses, organizations, and events portrayed in this book are entirely fictional or used fictitiously. Any resemblance to actual persons, living or dead, or to real businesses, events, or locales is purely coincidental.

To be clear: *Screwfix Academy* does not exist (though we admit it sounds like a solid institution), *Peter Trumper* is a wholly fictional creation, and the *Golden Poppadom restaurant* is a figment of the author's imagination—any similarities to your favorite curry spot are unintentional but flattering.

The *French Bistro in Station Road*? Also invented. And no, *Marcel Proust* never took tea there. Not once.

The author takes full responsibility for all imaginative liberties. Please enjoy accordingly.

DEDICATION

I'd like to dedicate this collection of stories to colleagues and others who have unwittingly inspired the characters and events therein. My wife deserves a mention too: she's had to put up with Peter Trumper almost as long as I have.

ACKNOWLEDGEMENTS

Finally, this collection benefits hugely from the wonderful support of the Fawcett Publications editorial team, led by Brian Emery and Mark Smith. Inventive, creative, critical when required to be, but wholehearted in their belief in Mr. Trumper.

TABLE OF CONTENTS

PREFACE

by Sebastian Bryant, M.A., Dip.Ed., former Headmaster, Screwfix Academy

I hold my hands up; the fault is mine. I appointed Peter Trumper to the school that is now known as Screwfix Academy and is sponsored by that well-known DIY chain.

Trumper is how we all referred to him. I've therefore taken the liberty of modifying all references to him in what you are about to read. Trumper it shall be!

At the time of his appointment, Peter seemed a strong candidate for the position of Head of French, which had become vacant following the retirement of the long-serving Tom Barley. Three of us interviewed him: our Chairman of Governors, Thelonius Moribund (of Moribund and Moribund Funeral Services Ltd.), Mrs Marjorie Nondescript (my Deputy Head), and myself. You'll appreciate that I've changed these names for reasons of discretion.

During his interview, Mr Trumper regaled us with his vast experience in other top schools, and before that his distinguished academic career at the University of Oxford as well as his sporting and social prowess.

His references were exemplary: an Oxford don and the headmaster of a major public school. They declared him a majestic scholar, tipped as a future professor, but passionate in his desire to devote himself to the classroom. He'd then been the outstanding pedagogue whose pupils' examination results far outstripped those of his colleagues, and who was hugely popular and greatly admired by pupils and fellow teachers alike. His contribution to extra-curricular activities was spectacular and enriching.

Sadly, the role of the internet in all of this cannot be ignored. I suspected at the time that something was amiss but couldn't say exactly what it was. I am now aware that services are available in the darker recesses of that spider's web which conventional morality might struggle to justify. Academic essays, certificates and diplomas, testimonials too can be purchased for a modest sum, with mock-up branding to appear just like the real thing. I must also admit that Peter was supremely self-confident, a fact which too often blinds us to the void which lies beneath.

Marjorie noted that he was well presented, smartly dressed, and wore an expensive aftershave. She was all for him. As her choice cancelled out mine, the Chairman had the casting vote and, like her, he was in favour.

After working at our school for just over five years, Mr Trumper is now deceased. The police treated his death, at the age of 43, as a possible murder, and several people were interviewed including myself and other colleagues. No arrest was made, and so far as I know the verdict remains open. My colleague Carol Jones has published an investigative paper on the matter entitled *The Body in the Graveyard*. I haven't found time to read it yet, but I would be surprised if it uncovers any fresh evidence.

Even before his death, many things became clear which at first had only been suspected. He had never attended the University of Oxford, apart from once at an open day. No proof emerged of his enthusiasm or aptitude for culture or sport. I heard his spoken French described as *'comme une vache espagnole,'* and no third party ever contradicted that rather frank indictment. Some pupils feared him; none admired him.

Something else emerged which I would never have guessed. Peter kept a diary during his time with us, and perhaps at other times too. His father, also called Peter, handed me the relevant pages after finding them when he was clearing out his son's old house. I suspect he never read them; if he had, he might sensibly have kept their contents to himself.

Those pages are presented to you now, albeit with slight amendments. I've removed references to his true name, so that Trumper he remains. I've changed the title and a few other details of the piece about his visit to the brothel, because it so reminded me of Gustave Flaubert. You may detect evidence of my hand elsewhere; I have, however, tried to keep my editorial impositions to a minimum. As for the tale involving Marcel Proust, I can add only that I was later introduced to the actor involved. I honestly believe that Mr Trumper thought he had met the real Proust and was unaware that the author of *A la recherche du temps perdu* died in 1922.

It may interest readers to know that my school received a second Ofsted inspection not long after the one which Mr Trumper describes. By then, Peter was no longer with us, but the inspectors' verdict was once again unfairly demoralising to my talented and hard-working staff. I was faced with little option but to retire; some colleagues also moved on, whilst others still work at the 'Academy' which we were forced to become.

Sebastian Bryant

Former Headmaster, Screwfix Academy

Mister Trumper's Christmas Carol

Barley was dead: to begin with. There is no doubt whatever about that. The register of his burial was signed by the clergyman, the clerk, the undertaker and the chief mourner. Old Barley was as dead as a doornail.

That's a sparkling introduction I've just written, and so original! What's more, it's true! Tom Barley retired as Head of French four years ago, at the end of the summer term, and at the good old age of 68. Mr Bryant, the headmaster, made a speech in his honour. A pompous, long-winded speech which paid fulsome tribute to the deadbeat old codger who was leaving but made only brief mention of me, Peter Trumper, the thrusting young blade who had been selected to replace him. Common sense would have set it the other way about.

And then, this October, Tom Barley had the misfortune to die most suddenly. During the night, his heart simply stopped beating, and when he woke up the next morning, he didn't, because he was dead. It's quite common among retired schoolmasters, especially ones who lived only for their job. Take that away and there's nothing left. No point in going on.

His death was the occasion for further tributes, and more pictures pinned up at school. I took down as many as I could, replacing them with photographs of myself – surrounded by pupils, alone, in school, out of school, posing for the camera or in natural mode. Almost immediately, they too vanished, and Tom Barley's face reappeared everywhere. This carried on for several weeks, until Christmas was nearly upon us.

I went home as usual after school that Friday. Checking to see that I wasn't being observed by Mr Laurels, my neighbour, or Mrs Snoop from next-door-but-one, I did something I love to do, for no other reason than because I have the technology to do it. I rang my own doorbell, then looked at my phone to see the doorbell-camera image of my handsome caller. I'm always struck by how closely I resemble Hugh Grant when he was a much younger man. Imagine my shock: the face that stared back at me was not my own, but Tom Barley's.

"Who are you? What do you want with me?" I gasped.

"Ask not who I am, but who I was," said the image. "But you know that already. What do I want? I want much with you, Mr Trumper."

"What are you doing here?" I asked. "Why aren't you in school? That's where everybody knew you."

"I do appear in school," said the figure, "but every image of me is taken down and thrown away. You're not going to throw away your mobile phone, though, are you?"

"It's nearly a year old," I said, "and I've been meaning to ask for an upgrade. My contract entitles me to one, you know."

"As you please, Mr Trumper. One phone or another, it makes no odds to me. But I cannot stay long. Over forty years working at that school, and now a constant wandering, nowhere to settle or call home."

"Well, don't let me keep you talking," I urged him. I was in quite a hurry to snuggle up inside, perhaps with a glass of the mulled wine which my mother had recently given me.

"I have just one message for you, Peter. If it is not too late, it may yet bring you redemption."

Already dark, the late afternoon air was damp and chilly. Around me, an eerie fog was closing in. It was no weather to be standing outside.

"Spit it out, then!" I called.

"You will be haunted," the ghost declared, "by three spirits. Expect the first tomorrow, when the clock strikes one."

Suddenly another much sharper voice startled me, but not as much as Tom Barley's had done.

"Mister Trumper! Is everything alright? You haven't lost your key, have you?" It was Mrs Snoop, my neighbour, who must have spotted me on the doorstep. How much of my ghostly conversation had she overheard?

"No, all fine," I replied. I made a pretence of searching my jacket and trousers. "I'd simply put it in the wrong pocket," I claimed. As I inserted it into the keyhole, the face from my mobile phone disappeared as suddenly as it had come.

Inside, I opted for a gin and tonic rather than a mulled wine. I switched on the television to distract me and was relieved to find my usual tea-time quiz show. But rather than calling out the answers ahead of the contestants, as I normally like to do, I found myself unable to focus on the presenter. One question alone was whirring through my mind. What had I really seen on my doorbell camera?

******

I had the impression of a restless night. Visions of pupils I'd taught (unruly ignoramuses), colleagues I'd barely tolerated, and swirling fog and snow. But when my alarm sounded, at the unexpected hour of one o'clock, I discovered I was asleep on the sofa, still fully dressed, and the television was blaring away to itself.

Someone else was in the room. A burglar, perhaps? I'd been so soundly asleep that I wouldn't have heard anyone come in, and by nodding off so suddenly, I'd omitted to set the intruder alarm.

Even in the semi-darkness, I recognised the figure. It was Lizzy Lee, my cleaning lady's daughter, and my most deplorable pupil at school. Not as she is now, the sixth former and university applicant, but as she was a couple of years ago. School uniform, short skirt, nice legs, and a developing bosom which her thin blouse barely concealed. Not as though I notice such things, of course. Each pupil, irrespective of how they look, is but an empty vessel to be filled with the pearls of my wisdom.

She beckoned me to follow. "To the public library, sir," she said. She always calls me 'sir,' but I don't think she means it with true deference, and I resent her for that.

"I was expecting the Ghost of Christmas Past," I reprimanded her.

"Not Christmas Past," she said, "but yours. One of the first A-Level pupils you taught. Remember Tony Caldwell?"

I did remember him. Dim-witted, slow on the uptake, a perpetual daydreamer, unresponsive to my wit. I suspected Tom Barley had admitted him to the sixth form only because he knew that since he was retiring, it would be someone else's misfortune to have to drum some intelligence into the young miscreant.

"I take it we're going to visit young Caldwell in the local prison?" I surmised.

"No, sir, I already told you, we're going to the public library," Lizzy replied.

I've never seen the point of libraries, and I think Lizzy was rubbing it in by taking me there. If I want a book, it can be for one of two reasons, both of which mean I want to keep it, not give it back after my allotted fortnight is up. Supposing, say, I want a set of Italian recipes: I'd need to have them available every time I decide to cook an Italian meal. Actually, that's not true; I'd need to show them to Mrs Lee, my charlady, so that she could prepare me one, or maybe make me a selection to keep in my freezer for future enjoyment. Or I might want a book to place prominently in my hallway so that visitors will see it and admire me as the type of person who reads Romantic poetry, for example.

A poster outside the library announced a 'meet-the-celebrity' session where Tony Caldwell would be signing copies of his new book. What was going on? Was he an author? As a pupil, he'd barely been able to write his name at the top of his homework! Still, here at the library, he'd have the opportunity to thank me in person for starting him off on the route to fame and fortune.

Lizzy led me in. At the front desk, a po-faced woman told me Tony's session had finished some twenty minutes earlier. I explained who I was, and the lady said she'd see whether he was still available. A moment later she came back to say he was in the staff room having a cup of tea and a chat with the other librarians.

We went through to the back room. Facially, Tony looked barely older than he did when he left school, although he was now thicker-set and more muscular. The two librarians who were with him said they needed to get back to work and, after pouring me a cup of tea, they sat down at a table on the far side of the room, punching numbers into their computers.

"Hello Tony," I greeted him, "I remember you from my sixth form class. They tell me you've written a book!"

"Ah, Mr Trumper, I remember you too," he replied. And so he should, I thought!

"It ought to be me writing a book," I told him. "It could be a collection of amusing incidents from my illustrious career – the stupid things pupils have said to me, some of their hilarious mistakes in tests, and the witty retorts I've made to them and their parents. It would be a best seller!"

"I'm sure you're right," he said. "Mine's about football – how I turned professional after university. Then my first season with the club."

"I went to a football match once," I said. "It was against Norwich. And I play a bit myself, of course. I recently took part in the staff versus pupils game. Of course, I was the man of the match."

I was able to bring Tony up to date with recent events at school, including the praise I'd received from Ofsted inspector George Roland, but after a few minutes, he said he needed to leave to attend a training session. I hadn't realised that footballers train in the evening! As we left the library, a group of young girls, 13- or 14-year-olds, approached us and clamoured for autographs. Graciously, I was happy to oblige! Once they'd gone, I asked Tony if he could let me have a signed copy of his book. He didn't have one on him, so I told him to drop it in at school next week. It would look quite impressive if a well-known footballer and author turned up at the office and asked the receptionists, "Please would you make sure this is passed on to Mister Trumper?"

I realised I'd left my scarf behind, and asked Lizzy if we could pop back into the library to collect it. It was there on the desk, but as I picked it up, I overheard the two librarians talking.

"That man who was in," one said, "the schoolmaster, Mr Trumper."

"What about him?" the other asked.

"Not a word about Tony," the first one replied. "All about himself. How he should write his best-selling memoirs, the man of the match, the top teacher; no mention of Tony being Championship player of the season, on thirty grand a week, and a best-selling author."

"True," the other said, "and when that group of girls came around at the end, he thought it was his autograph they were all after! Not a clue that they all wanted Tony, twenty years younger, handsome, millionaire .... They say he'll play for England one day."

"Lizzy," I said to my ghostly companion, "remove me from this place. Take me home. Haunt me no longer."

"I shall make your visual reacquaintance at a subsequent juncture," she said. I'm sure she was saying it to rile me – that's one of Bryant's sayings, the pompous old fool! But at that point, I didn't care. Overcome by drowsiness, I trudged up the stairs to my bedroom – and undressed this time. My gin and tonic stood untouched on the table, and a heavy sleep once again overcame me.

******

I was woken not by any sound, but by a light shining into the room. My bedroom door was ajar, and the glow came from downstairs. Had someone entered while I was asleep, or had I left the light on when coming upstairs to bed?

In my downstairs room (the drawing room, as I like to call it) the light was indeed on, and sitting in my armchair was a somewhat spectral version of Bob Simpson. Mr Simpson joined the school at the same time as me, as a mere teacher, when I was appointed Head of Department. He lacks my talent and charisma; as for his ability in French, well, I like to tell pupils and other teachers alike that he's probably never even been to France. By 'spectral,' I mean that he seemed larger than in life, yet less solid, as if a sword or arrow could have pierced straight through him and emerged without drawing blood.   Another ghost, then, as I had been forewarned.

"Not Lizzy this time, then," I challenged him. "But Christmas Present, I take it?"

"The present, yes," he replied. "But Lizzy, as you persist in calling her, is too young for tonight's excursion."

"Will we be in danger?" I asked.

"None at all," he answered, "But as a 17-year-old, Izzy shouldn't be seen in licenced premises.   Not under our supervision, at any rate."

"We're going to a bar?" I surmised.   "Is it local? Is it one I know?"

This time, he offered no reply but summoned me to follow.   Our journey was short but eventful.   In the space of a few moments, I was fully dressed and had grabbed my wallet from the sideboard, and Bob had reverted to his usual form: squat, solid and slightly shorter than me.

The pub was called the Flying Duck, not an establishment I frequent.   Posters outside advertised 'Comedy Nite,' although I couldn't imagine any famous names from television coming to perform in such a modest venue. On the way in, Bob was greeted by a woman in her late twenties, slightly younger than him, I'd have guessed.   They spoke briefly in French – I didn't catch what they said, they spoke too quickly. Then he made the introductions: "Florence – my colleague Peter Trumper. Peter, this is Florence, my partner. We met in Bordeaux, when I was working there."

"*Enchanté, mademoiselle*," I greeted her. I had no idea that Bob had a partner, let alone an attractive young Frenchwoman!

"Pleased to meet you," she replied. "But no need for French tonight, we can speak English." How very rude! Everybody knows my French is far better than Bob's.

"You won't know Harry Bergson," Bob explained. "He's an English teacher, Flo's colleague. It's his début tonight. Performs under the name of Bill Bergson."

We found a table. The event was well attended, some customers sitting close to the stage and others standing around the perimeter. Drinks arrived: a glass of my favourite *Pinot Grigio*, a pint of beer for Bob, and a sparkling water for Florence.

"*Vous ne boivez pas vin ou bière?*" I fluently asked her.

"No, it's my turn to drive home," she said.

The first act was introduced. I say 'act' – he clearly wasn't a natural comedian. An elderly chap, he rambled on about the good old days – an age of neighbourliness, warmth and respect, so he claimed.

He had nothing but praise for the local policeman, or 'village bobby' as he was known, who used to give youngsters a 'cuff round the ear' which stopped them becoming career criminals. He even argued that National Service should be re-introduced for today's feckless youth. I wanted to tell him he was wrong on that score, because according to an article I'd read in *The Daily Mail*, the army wants skilled men, not gormless timewasters. But, uncharacteristically for me, I couldn't think of a witty response on the spur of the moment. Instead, I waited with rising impatience for his litany of outdated nonsense to drag to a close. The audience gave him a polite round of applause, which was more than he deserved.

Harry – introduced by the landlord as Bill Bergson – was next on the stage. I'd stood up to go to the bar, since Bob must have bought the first round of drinks, but he motioned me to sit down. I noticed that our drinks were still full, even though I'd definitely drunk over half of mine. You had to, listening to that first act!

I didn't pay much attention to Harry's comedy routine. I couldn't have cared less about his jokes, no matter how clever they might have been. What irritated me was the fact that a junior teacher, a man younger than myself, was standing in the spotlight feasting on the laughter and applause. Yet I – more accomplished and far more deserving of recognition – could only sit quietly by, a mere spectator. The injustice of it weighed heavily upon me.

When Harry's turn was over, he sat down at our table, still catching his breath. Bob and Florence congratulated him. Neither of them would have enjoyed addressing an audience of fifty-plus complete strangers, they said. I felt their praise was too enthusiastic, when all he'd done was to tell a few jokes for ten minutes. No big deal, and if he'd been nervous, he shouldn't have agreed to do it in the first place. My advice to him would be to stick to the day job, and not hog the limelight which should be kept for those of us who truly deserve it.

We were joined by another man who spoke to Harry first. "Well done," he said, going on to say how much he'd enjoyed one joke in particular – one which I hadn't found remotely funny, although I'd certainly have told it much better myself.

"Thank you," Harry said. Turning to us, he added, "This is Chris, he's organised this evening's entertainment. Chris, my colleague Florence, her partner Bob, and Bob's colleague Peter."

"I'm actually Bob's line manager," I corrected him. It had annoyed me when Bob introduced me to Florence as a mere colleague, when in truth I'm his boss. Now Harry too was denying me the deference my position deserved.

"Enjoying it so far?" Chris asked me.

"Not really," I replied. "It should be me up there on stage. I'm famous for my witty comments at school."

"You'd be most welcome next time," Chris said, handing me a business card. "Just ring me on this number and I'm sure we can fit you in."

"I'd expect a larger audience for my *bons mots*," I objected. "And a star presenter to introduce me, to give me a big build-up. A band, too, to play as I walk out onto the stage."

Chris smiled. "This is just an amateur night," he explained. "It's not intended for the big names. But you'd be welcome to join us."

I dismissed the idea. "Oh, in that case, I'm definitely cut out for something much bigger," I proclaimed.

The evening promised nothing but more of the same, a succession of lacklustre amateur comedians and their stale, weary patter. I told Bob I'd head for home. I'd done my duty by supporting his partner's colleague, and I didn't want to waste any more of my time. Bob offered to drive me; he also told his companions he'd return to the pub in a few minutes.

I recalled the two librarians gossiping behind my back, accusing me of not showing enough interest in Tony Caldwell's career. On the way home, I made a point of asking Bob about Harry Bergson's prospects as a comedian.

"He'll do more gigs," Bob replied, "but he'll get more into writing – stage comedies, TV sitcoms. That's where he'll make his money, I think, rather than as a performer."

I had no way of knowing whether Bob was foreseeing the future or simply guessing his friend's intentions, so I dropped the subject. I asked what guise my third spirit would take on; he either didn't know or wouldn't tell me.

******

No sooner had Bob disappeared when, lifting my eyes, I beheld a solemn phantom, draped and hooded, coming like a mist along the ground towards me. It was shrouded in a deep black garment which concealed its head and face. Yet from its ponderous manner, it was obvious to me that it was Sebastian Bryant, my headmaster.

"Am I in the presence of the Ghost of Christmas Yet To Come?" I asked. Astonishingly, the phantom made no reply. Bryant usually rambles on at great length when asked a simple question.

I tried again. "You are about to show me things which have not happened, but will happen in the future," I suggested. Again, no reply.

"Actually," I said, "I know where this is going. I've read *Ebenezer Scrooge* by Charles Dickens, and I know you're going to show me my own funeral. You'll expect me to feel sorry for myself, because I haven't had the recognition I truly deserved in life.

Well, tell me this. How long will I live? How old will I be when I die?"

This time, the phantom spoke. "We cannot predict the unpredictable," it said. "None of us knows how long he will live or when he will die. But tonight, we are not attending a funeral. Quite the reverse: a celebration!"

"Bob Simpson predicted Harry Bergson's future," I objected. "He said he'd be more successful as a writer than a performer."

"I know. An elementary prediction to make, based on Harry's knowledge, talent, ambition and determination," Bryant replied. "If you crave recognition and success, develop those qualities first."

I know I'm far more talented than Harry Bergson, and everybody else I work with too, so I changed the subject.

"The other spirits took me somewhere," I said. "Will you do that?"

"I shall indeed," he answered. "Prepare to visit Oxford!"

"Ah yes, Oxford, my student days," I recalled. "Happy times, the Boat Race, rowing on the River Ox, then a glass of sherry before dining at the Captain's table. Exams, too – and celebrating full marks in my degree."

"Peter," he growled, "we both know full well that you went nowhere near the University of Oxford."

I could not tell how we travelled. I was aware of foggy landscapes floating past, but in what seemed no more than a couple of minutes, we were sweeping in through the magnificent gates of what looked like a stately home but was in fact a 'college,' as the University of Oxford likes to call its different divisions. We took our places in the audience in a grand chamber with oak panelling and mullioned windows. In front of us, an elderly professor in a bow tie and a university gown stood at a lectern.

"Thank you all for finding the time to come here this evening," he began. "It is, as we all know, two hundred years since the first publication, in the *Revue de Paris*, of a novel which was to change the course of European literature. We are privileged in that tonight's speaker is one of the world's great authorities on that novel and its author. Please welcome Professor Lee."

I was in something of a panic, fretting that I was going to be announced as the speaker – a world-renowned expert, a privilege to listen to, it certainly sounded that way. But I couldn't think of any novel that was two hundred years old, a difficulty which was compounded by the fact that I didn't know how far into the future we'd travelled. The novel might be *Harry Potter* for all I knew!

As the lecturer appeared, my fear subsided, only to be replaced by sheer astonishment. She looked exactly like my charlady, Mrs Lee! A smartened up version in an academic gown, but her, nonetheless. The elderly gentleman stood aside, and she was applauded as she replaced him behind the lectern.

From the first words of her talk, I gathered that the novel was called *Madame Boovaroo*, by Gustav Flubber, published in 1856. The year must now be 2056, I calculated, and Mrs Lee must therefore be well into her seventies. Then it dawned on me – Professor Lee was my former pupil, Lizzy Lee, my cleaner's daughter. Bryant leant over to me.

"You remember how proud we all were when the school produced its first ever Oxford undergraduate?" he whispered. "Who would have thought she'd go on to become our first ever Oxford professor?"

I didn't follow much of the speech, although the rest of the audience listened politely enough and gave another generous round of applause when she stood down some forty minutes later. She invited questions, some of which came in French; when they were, then it was in French that she answered them. I must admit I never cared for the girl when she was at school, but I was proud to think that whatever she'd achieved in adult life was all thanks to me.

The evening – which, according to posters outside, had been organised by the International Flaubert Society – finished with sherry being served in the 'JCR,' which I thought was a kind of bulldozer but was in fact another intricately carved oak-panelled room where servants flitted about offering drinks from silver trays. It stands for Junior Common Room, I discovered, and is the hub of student cultural and social life. But at least I was right about the sherry!

Finally, the evening showed signs of drawing to a close. Several guests, having finished their drinks and expressed their appreciation to the speaker, were starting to drift away. I'd just taken a second glass of sherry when the professor who had introduced the event approached me. To my surprise, I realised that he bore an uncanny resemblance to Tom Barley.

"An excellent lecture, don't you think?" he asked me. "It goes to show, no matter how well you think you know your Flaubert, there's always more to learn."

"I wasn't impressed," I answered. "Maybe if you'd never heard of *Madame Boovaroo*, you might have picked up a fact or two, but for those of us who know it well, it was all very familiar."

"Hardly," he said. "It's amazing what new research is still finding out, even two hundred years on."

"Actually," I countered, "I'm sure I've heard that very same lecture before. It must happen a lot — each professor writes a few lectures and then sells them on to others. Then every year they each read them out to their own students. A bit like vicars with their sermons.”

“You know,” he said, “ours must be the luckiest profession. We spend our lives surrounded by students and colleagues with so much potential and such greater talent than our own. They have everything to teach us.”

“That can’t be true,” I pointed out. “In my whole career, I’ve not encountered a pupil with even a fraction of my ability.”

“An England international football captain? A BAFTA winning comedy writer? An Oxford professor?” he suggested.

“Oh, I suppose everyone has some skill in their own way,” I admitted, “But remember, it was me who started them out on their paths to success. I couldn’t have done that if my talent was less than theirs!”

He tried to argue, but I wasn’t having it. I finished my sherry and looked round for old Bryant to take me home. But as he emerged towards me, I saw an alteration in his hood and dress. He shrank, collapsed and dwindled down into a bedpost.

******

And the bedpost was my own! The bed, and the room, were my own. And it was 8:30 on Saturday morning. The spirits must all have come and departed within one night!

Saturday meant I could expect Mrs Lee, my charlady. I determined to be up and dressed before she arrived. She could still cook me my breakfast before she started her cleaning duties, but she couldn't accuse me of being a stay-a-bed. And I had so much to do!

I re-watched *Scrooge* by Charles Dickens, or at least the ending. I was right: Scrooge is given a foresight of his own funeral, after which he reforms, and it all ends happily. But Scrooge is quite mean, and nobody really likes him – the complete opposite to me. So, what message could there possibly be in what I now realised had been a dream, although it all felt real enough at the time?

My flaw, I realised, is that I'm too modest for a man who's accomplished so much. I speak superb French, probably better than most Frenchmen, and I'm talented in German and Italian too. I was highly praised by George Roland after our school's Ofsted inspection. I could tell you about my successful appearance on the BBC's *Mastermind* quiz show or the exciting visit I organised to France for my pupils. Despite Bryant's scepticism, most people willingly believe me when I tell them that I studied at Oxford University. And if Lizzy Lee gets a place there too, I hope she'll remember how I set her on the path to success, just as I did for Harry Bergson in comedy and Tony Caldwell in his sporting career.

How, then, could my accomplishments be given the recognition they truly deserve? Ideally, I suppose, a film would be my perfect tribute, although that raises the question of who could successfully portray me on screen. Hugh Grant is far too old now, as are the various actors who've played James Bond, and the younger ones are more used to fantasy and science fiction than to true-life biography.

Instead, it will have to be a book, then, a collection of my memoirs which I shall start to write as soon as possible, maybe even later today. I do hope you'll enjoy them.

The Curious Incident of the Pupils who were too Clever

I've already referred to Mr Bryant, the pompous old fool who struts around as our Headmaster. The wordy old windbag who never uses one word when a hundred will do. I should also mention Marjorie, our Deputy Head, who's even more pointless than he is. I've never heard her speak; she's always there in School Assembly with her clipboard, noting which members of staff are present and which aren't, and I'm told her only other purpose is to arrange for 'cover' when teachers are absent. 'Cover' means emailing another teacher to babysit for the lesson, or in an extreme situation, booking a supply teacher from an agency. The first of those costs the school nothing; the second incurs a fee, of course.

But I haven't yet spoken about the third member of our 'cushy jobs brigade,' or 'senior management' as they like to style themselves. He's Mr Aspinall, a superannuated art teacher who always seems to be going on courses. "So what?" I say, but when he comes back from a course, he invariably brings some new 'initiative,' as he likes to call it, and then we pay lip-service to this new-fangled nonsense for a few weeks until he goes on another course and comes back with something completely different but equally worthless.

As our drama teacher, 'Luvvie' Laithwaite, always says, "There goes another initiative, back to the pavilion, without troubling the scorers." I'm told that's a cricketing expression, although I don't fully understand why.

This time, the initiative was called 'The Critical Buddy.' We were to pair up, one teacher with another, and watch what our colleague did, in class, in meetings, in the staffroom or wherever. Then we had to write a report in which, as a 'friend,' we were to give praise for what our associate did well, but as a 'critical friend,' we had to point out things which he or she could do better. Politely, of course. We were given 48 hours to hand in the name of our chosen partner to Mr Aspinall's office which, in keeping with his status, is smaller than Mr Bryant's or Marjorie's but slightly larger than the cubicle in the staff toilet.

I confidently expected a flood of applicants to be my partner for the exercise. Whoever I selected would enjoy the opportunity to watch my superb teaching, followed by the privilege of receiving my judgement of his work, with expert pointers to instruct him in how to make his classes more like my own.

The deadline passed, however, and of applicants there were none.

Aspinall caught me in the dinner hall and asked me what efforts I'd made to nab a partner. A partner in his initiative, he naturally meant, and not a partner in matrimony! I told him I'd been much too busy, and besides, it should be up to others to solicit a partnership with me, and not vice versa. I shouldn't be the one to go round cap in hand, I told him. He said he'd approached several colleagues on my behalf, but they'd all declined. I'd therefore have to be my own 'Critical Buddy' and write my own review so that the figures balanced in case we had an inspection visit from Ofsted.

At first, I thought this was one of the worst 'box-ticking exercises' I'd ever come across, but the more I considered it, the more I realised I could turn it to my advantage. My 'critical buddy,' which would of course be me, could praise my qualities at length. Bryant would have to accept it, and if Ofsted did descend on us, they'd have to acknowledge it too.

Strangely enough, the idea put me in mind of Sherlock Holmes. As a boy, I'd been given a book one Christmas entitled *The Adventures of Sherlock Holmes, Abridged for Younger Readers*. I liked the way that Sherlock Holmes's cases were narrated by his companion Doctor Watson, who was obviously a big admirer of Holmes. Perhaps I could be my own 'Doctor Watson,' reporting on my special adventures.

When I was older, I found in the school library some of the Sherlock Holmes stories in the unabridged version, the way they were originally written. I didn't enjoy them at all! The language was so complicated, so overdone, that they really made no sense whatsoever. "Pray continue your narrative, my dear Watson," Sherlock Holmes would say. Or else, "I entreat you to relate the singular occurrence which has befallen you, la di dah!"

Nobody talks like that nowadays, apart from Mr Bryant, of course.

But I finished my 'Critical Buddy's Report,' and I felt quite proud of it. In the absence of another author, I decided to attribute it to John Crick, from the Maths department. Apart from myself, he's probably the most intelligent member of staff at our school, being the only one with a Ph D. Here is what I wrote:

*****

"How honoured I was, Headmaster, to be allocated Mr Peter Trumper as my companion for this excellent and wonderful initiative. His reputation goes before him; admiring pupils and subordinates dub him 'Mister French' for his supreme mastery of the French language and culture. His prowess far outstrips that of his lesser colleagues – I shan't name names, but I could suggest Mr Simpson, who has probably never even been to France! By contrast, when Mr Trumper visits the country, as he so often does, he is greeted there as a native! Why, on hearing his wonderful command of the French language, everyone who falls under his considerable charm simply presumes that he must be French.

"I know too of his status as an upholder of high standards, a disciplinarian. Any pupil who crosses him knows that he, or she, will immediately be made to feel very small indeed.

"So, then, I, John H Crick, a Doctor of Mathematics, entered the staffroom one morning to find Peter Trumper ensconced in an armchair. He had just finished *The Times* crossword, and he greeted me with the words, "A straightforward puzzle today, my dear Crick." As he slipped the folded newspaper into his elegant Italian leather briefcase, his wise, perceptive eyes lingered on me for a moment, and he added, "Now, my good man, I observe that you are without your motor car this morning."

""Great heavens, Trumper," I ejaculated, "How the devil did you know that?"

""Elementary," he declared, "The dampness on your clothes tells me you have but recently entered the building. Yet there is no mud on your shoes, which would have come from that area of the car park where you standard grade teachers are allowed to leave your vehicles. I therefore deduce that you arrived by bus and walked down the school drive from the main gate."

""Brilliant, Trumper," I averred. "And I suppose now you're going to tell me what's wrong with my car, too?"

""Only its great age and high mileage," Mr Trumper opined. "You should be more like me – I change my car every twelve months. I always opt for the top-of-the-range model, and that way I get the best trade-in value at the end of the year. Let that be your first lesson of the morning. By the way, I gather your wife is temporarily away – visiting relatives, perhaps?"

""Yes, she is – her mother's had another turn; she's taking her to the hospital. But how could you tell?"

""Because she omitted to make your packed lunch this morning," Trumper explained. "The smear on your cuff could not possibly have come from your breakfast. And if you regularly prepared your own sandwiches, you would surely be in the habit of rolling your sleeves up beforehand. Egg and mayonnaise, I surmise."

"I had to concede that he was right, as always. I wanted to discuss with him how our partnership might develop to our mutual benefit, but his agile mind was already ahead of me.

""But you have a more pressing concern than your poor, cheap motor and your wife's ailing mother," he intuited. "Yesterday you set your class a test, which you marked last night. The abnormally high scores led you to suspect that several of your pupils must have been cheating, and yet you cannot understand how."

""That's exactly it," I confessed. "Have you been following me?"

""There's no need for that, my dear Crick." Mr Trumper's fine, handsome features formed themselves into a kindly but knowing smile, and I was reminded of just how closely he resembled a younger version of Hugh Grant, the celebrated English actor. He continued, "Your briefcase is bulging with papers. Regular homework would have waited until the weekend – this was a test, therefore. Sets of right or wrong answers would have been quickly despatched and the scores entered in your mark book. However, the rings under your eyes tell me you worked long into the evening – your pupils did well, but you cannot fathom how they achieved so highly."

""Your powers are remarkable," I observed, "but what can I do? How can I catch the cheats?"

"Trumper asked me which class it was, and I told him. It was the top set in Year 10, a group of around thirty 14- and 15-year-olds.

""Precisely the class which I myself shall be teaching after morning break," he informed me. "An idle, deviant set of little wastrels if ever I knew one, you mark my words. Come into my class with me at 11 o'clock. Not only will you have the privilege of seeing one of the truly superb lessons for which I am rightly renowned, but I shall point out the guilty party before your very eyes."

"I eagerly anticipated Mr Trumper's class, having heard many reports of his wonderful lessons, and was queuing with the pupils outside the classroom well before he arrived. He came swishing along the corridor with cries of "Make way! Make way!" and unlocked the door. In we went, the youngsters stepping aside for me as they perhaps assumed I had business with him before the lesson started. The boys and girls found their way to their seats whilst I hovered, waiting for a vacant spot to be indicated to me. But as the children filed through the doorway, Trumper placed himself in front of the last one to enter the room, effectively blocking his route.

""You, young man!" he bellowed, "What's the meaning of this?"

""Wha – what?" the boy stammered.

""Don't say 'what' to me," Mr Trumper roared. "The word is 'I beg your pardon'."

""I – I beg your pardon," the little wretch repeated, looking quite crestfallen.

""I beg your pardon what?" Trumper growled.

""That's what I said, I said 'I beg your pardon'," the child tried to say.

""You mean, 'I beg your pardon, SIR!'" Mr Trumper insisted.

""Yes, please, your pardon, sir," the poor whelp stuttered.

""That's better. And don't you ever be late for my lesson again. My lessons are the most precious gift you'll ever receive in this school, and I'm not having you taking them lightly. Should you repeat your offence, you'll find your life is simply not worth living, if indeed it ever was. Now get to your place at once!"

"I have to say that, as he often reminds us, Mr Trumper is not a man to be thwarted.

"I looked for a spare seat for myself but couldn't readily see one. Trying to remain inconspicuous in the corner, I felt uncomfortable for the poor boy who'd been singled out for the sharp end of Mr Trumper's tongue. The lad himself, on the other hand, didn't seem unduly perturbed, and a girl near me whispered in my direction, "He always does that – whoever comes in last gets slated. We take it in turns."

""We're joined today by my colleague Doctor Crick," Mr Trumper announced to the class. "He's come to see what a truly excellent lesson looks like. In a moment, he and I will have a brief word in the corridor. In the meantime, we shall start with a test. Take a sheet of paper and write down the names of ten fruits and ten vegetables, in French, from the vocabulary list on page 46 of *Sacré Bleu!*"

"Then he turned to me. "Doctor Crick, a word, if you please," and gestured me to follow him into the corridor.

"I could appreciate the cunning of his clever trick. He'd set the pupils a test but had given them the opportunity to cheat while his back was turned. Any one of them could easily take his textbook, turn to page 46, and copy out a list of French fruits and vegetables. That would expose the fraudster! However, when we re-entered the classroom, it was obvious that most of them had the book open under their desk and were transcribing what they found there. He ignored their artifice, and we both patrolled the room, looking over the shoulders of the learners as they wrote.

"Most were producing the expected fare: *une pomme, une banane, une orange, des pommes de terre, des carottes, des haricots*. One poor mite had his book open at the wrong page, and was copying: *les pneus, le pare-brise, le moteur*. A girl who clearly wasn't cheating because she had a closed textbook on the table in front of her had written a different list from the others, which ran: *des betteraves, des asperges, de la rémoulade*. Mr Trumper seized upon this girl.

""You, what on earth is this?" he demanded, "And what's your name? Why haven't you written it at the top of the page?"

""That's Izzy," I said. I could see how she probably got under Mr Trumper's skin; I knew her to be a bright girl, if a touch eccentric. "Izzy Lee," I added.

""Ah yes, Lizzy," he insisted. "Of course I know her. Her mother happens to be my charlady, my domestic cleaner. But what's this rubbish you've written, Lizzy?"

"Sir," she explained, "*Betteraves* is beetroot, *asperges* is asparagus, and *la rémou* – "

""No, that's not French at all," he exclaimed, "I've never heard of any of them. And I know every word in the French language. So, if I don't know it, it doesn't exist."

"The girl might foolishly have wanted to challenge Mr Trumper's authority, but at that point, he instructed the class to put their pens down. The pupil who had been accused of arriving late was told to collect in the papers, which Mr Trumper assured them he would mark before their next class. He then stage-whispered to me, "In their dreams – they're for the bin, *wha, wha, wha!*"

"As ever, his wit was truly astounding, but I still could not understand how this would reveal how the same pupils had cheated in their Maths test the other day. There was no list of answers in their Maths textbook, and I'd been with them in the classroom throughout. But at this point, the brilliance of Mr Trumper's teaching started to overwhelm me. He immediately set out the aims of today's class. Of course, as always, his lesson was superbly planned, but now he also demonstrated his flexibility as he modified his objectives with my dilemma in mind.

"'"Today," he explained, "I'm going to teach you how to answer Question 7 in the GCSE syllabus, *Quelle est la profession de tes parents?* By the end of the lesson, you will all be able to say, in French, what both your father and your mother do for a living."

"This seemed to me an attainable goal, although I wondered about the pupils who had only one parent, and who might therefore have to say, "My father ran off with a barmaid," or those who might be ashamed on behalf of parents who were unemployed. Mr Trumper resumed.

"'"Very well," said he. "Now the French for 'My father is' is '*Mon père est* ....','" and he proceeded to write this on the whiteboard. "'My mother is' is '*Ma mère est* ....' But you need to say, 'AND my mother is ....' I don't suppose any of you ignoramuses can tell me the French word for 'and'."

"A few intrepid souls raised their hands, but Mr Trumper would have none of it. "As I suspected, of course you can't," he declaimed. "The French for 'and' is the word '*et*'." He then wrote on the board the phrase '*et ma mère est* ....' "Now," he instructed, "using your dictionaries, you have ten minutes to copy down and complete the sentence '*Mon père est* ...... *et ma mère est* ......' in your own words. Go on, or as we say in French, *Allez sur!*"

"As a teacher of Mathematics, I don't know a great deal of French, but I could see how this might work if everyone's parents had easy-to-define professions, such as fireman, cook or electrician. But how to cope with the unexpected? Sure enough, many of the class put their hands up with all kinds of questions: "Sir, what's a software designer?" "What's a project manager?" "How do you say 'Self-employed'?"

"Assured as ever, Mr Trumper had the definitive answer to every one of their queries. "Software designer, that's *'Artiste de produit doux.'* Project manager, that's *'Directeur de projet.'* Self-employed, that's *'Employé de …'* oh, never mind, just say *'Employé'*."

"Remarkably, his extensive vocabulary stretched to even the most specialised of professions – plumbers, shop assistants, car mechanics, secretaries. I was bowled over by his pronunciation of *ingénieur* (engineer) and *infirmière* (nurse) – so very French! Not once did he need to turn to his own pocket dictionary, hidden behind his desk! On finding the word *esthéticienne* (a girl had asked him the French for beautician), he wisely adjudicated that it would be too hard for her to pronounce, so he declined to read it out, and suggested she use *une femme de beauté* instead.

""I presume she works in a massage parlour," he sneered. "Well, we all know what goes on in those establishments! Please don't write down the extras she offers her clients, *wha, wha, wha!*"

"Mr Trumper's lightning repartee was too slick for the girl, and she looked suitably downcast. Like the latecomer, she wouldn't be causing trouble again that lesson. The questions died down and the pupils set unwillingly to their task, determined no doubt that it should take them the full ten minutes that Mr Trumper had allotted. I moved up and down the aisles, pausing behind Izzy Lee to see what she had written. *"Mon père est mort quand j'étais petite,"* it ran. *"Ma mère fait de son mieux pour moi. Elle travaille comme femme de ménage chez des cons et des salauds."* I knew that wouldn't find favour with Mr Trumper, and hoped he wouldn't see it.

"The truth dawned on me, as Mr Trumper had surely known it would, when we paused behind Claire, whom I knew to be an obedient and assiduous girl, if not overly bright. Something of a disappointment to her parents, I feared, as I knew they had academic ambitions for her which she would be unlikely ever to fulfil. On her page was written, *"Je m'appelle Claire Martin. Mon père est avocat et ma mère est professeur de mathématique."* Everything clicked into place, as it had for Mr Trumper before me.

""Tell me, Claire, does your mother teach Year 10 Maths?" he asked her.

""I think so, sir, she might," the girl answered.

""I presume she has a copy of the Teacher's Handbook to accompany GCSE Foundation Maths for Schools?"

""I don't know, sir. I've never seen it."

""You must have seen it. It's a blue book, isn't it?" he prompted.

""No, sir, it's green. It's the pupil's book that's blue."

"I don't think the girl realised she'd given herself away. Mr Trumper pressed home his advantage.

""So, on Monday night, you scanned the test that Doctor Crick was going to give you on Tuesday. And the answers page. Then you went on Twitter and sent both pages to everyone in the class. Do you use Twitter?" he asked. She giggled, I presume because Twitter is seen as out of date by her age group, but he sternly repeated the question.

""No, sir, I use Instagram and WhatsApp," she confessed.

""There we have it. Give Doctor Crick your phone."

"I took Claire's phone and put it in my coat pocket. I felt sorry for her – she wasn't a natural cheat, and she certainly wasn't an accomplished liar. Obtaining an advance copy of the test was probably her way of trying to secure a mark that would keep her demanding parents happy until the next disappointment came along. Passing it on must have been an attempt to curry favour with her classmates. I knew I would have to impose a punishment, as the poor girl had broken the rules, but I understood why she'd done it.

"Mr Trumper took the high ground. "For me, the matter is closed," he declared. "From now on, it is between Doctor Crick and yourself."

"Mr Trumper brought his class to an end with his usual consummate skill. He announced that the next lesson would start with each pupil reciting to him, from memory, their answer to today's question, and it would be followed by a further test in which they would be required to write, in French, the names of ten jobs or professions. And there would be no copying from page 54 of *Sacré Bleu!*; they would all be told to leave their textbooks by the door as they entered the classroom.

"I left Mr Trumper after the lesson. He was heading back to the staffroom; I had another class to teach.

"But we met a couple of days later for our 'debriefing.' I love the way these military terms have been adopted into our schoolteachers' vocabulary: 'briefing' and 'debriefing', along with 'targets,' 'aims and objectives,' 'residuals' and 'collateral.' It makes us sound so macho, so SAS.

"I was, of course, wholly in awe of Mr Trumper's command of his classroom and his subject matter. It puts the rest of us to shame! If only we all could be more like him! I'm sure he has a special talent which is beyond the scope of us mere mortals. He promised to attend one of my classes in the near future, and I would feel doubly honoured if he could find the time in his busy schedule – after all, many other colleagues must also be soliciting his wise counsel.

"Nonetheless, he allocated me a generous proportion of his time – almost five minutes – to remind me that for him the exceptional was the norm, and to reassure me that my own modest efforts were probably just as good as any of his lesser colleagues could achieve.

"Should Ofsted descend upon us, I know that they, too, would relish the experience that Mister Trumper has graciously allowed me to enjoy today.

"Signed, Doctor John H Crick, 15 May."

*****

Along with everybody else, I handed in my report to Mr Aspinall at the end of the week. He must have passed them on to Mr Bryant (probably because with the number of us on the staff, there wasn't room for so many pieces of paper in his office). The following week, Mr Bryant told me in the staffroom how much he'd enjoyed my writing, adding that in Sherlock Holmes's opinion, Doctor Watson's records also 'occasionally embellished the details of certain of his cases'. The report 'showed promise,' he thought, and he would 'peruse it in greater detail at a subsequent juncture,' which is a favourite phrase of his.

Les Vacances de Monsieur Trumper

I sometimes think a film would be a wonderful tribute to my achievements. None more so than my visit to France. But it would take quite some actor to portray me! Given our resemblance, Hugh Grant might have taken on the role when he was a lot younger than he is today.

Of course, travel is always fraught with peril. The temporary loss of my passport was a mystery. I'm sure I had it in the coach when we left school, and I'm always right about such matters.

In Dover, a port official stepped on board to say that just one person should go to passport control. That's the only time I left my seat – to collect the passports from the 30-odd pupils who had been selected to accompany me.

At the desk, I introduced myself to the officer. "Peter Trumper, Head of Modern Languages. *Enchanté, Madame.*" I waited patiently while she perused the documents. I lightened the tone with a witty remark, saying we'd decided not to bring Osama Bin Laden with us on this trip, but she failed to appreciate my quickfire humour. All she said was, "Very good, sir. And your own passport?"

In my haste, I'd left it on the coach. When I went back, it wasn't there. It should have been in the inside pocket of my jacket which hung from a hook above the coach window. I returned to the customs shed.

"I seem to have misplaced it," I explained, "I'm sure it will turn up."

"I'm sorry, sir," she mumbled, "but rules are rules. No passport, no trip to France."

Fortunately, I was well prepared for this scenario, unexpected though it was. Not only do I speak perfect French, but I'd also taken care to dress in French style for the occasion. My slacks were a couple of inches shorter than I'd normally wear them – I'd seen this in a French film, *Mr Hulot's Holiday* starring Jacques Tati – so I showed an enticing glimpse of sock, and I was wearing a blue and white striped jersey purchased specially for the occasion. I'd also bought a *béret*, but I wasn't planning to reveal that until we arrived in France.

"My good woman," I said, "I need to accompany my party to France. When we arrive, as soon as the authorities hear my superb French, they'll quite naturally welcome me as a true Frenchman."

"And if I let you go with no passport," she persisted, "how would you return to the UK?"

"Well, that's obvious," I replied. "You've seen me. You know I'm British. You know perfectly well I'm entitled to come back to my own country."

"That's not how it works," she claimed, adding a "sir" in a tone that I might almost have considered disdainful.

"I demand to see your superior," I told her.

"My superior would arrest you for attempting to exit the UK illegally," she threatened. "Your colleagues and your pupils can go to France, but you're staying here. In custody or not, the choice is yours."

One of her fellow-officers accompanied me back onto the coach. I told my two colleagues what had happened and how I'd been so unfairly treated by the jobsworth minions. Strangely, they didn't seem particularly surprised or disappointed. I took my wallet from my inside pocket – the jacket was still hanging where I'd left it – and passed some of the money over to them. Then, taking my bags from the overhead shelves, I got back off the coach.

At that point I thought a silent movie might be the best *genre*, as we French speakers say, to do justice to my adventures. Admittedly, my quip about Osama Bin Laden would be lost. But my forlorn expression as I watched the coach being waved through towards the ferry would tug at the heart strings like Charlie Chaplin, although I'm taller, better looking and more elegantly dressed, of course.

But what had happened to my passport? I normally have outstanding detective skills – essential for when pupils try to deceive me over missing homework and various other misdemeanours – but this truly had me wondering. It can't have been theft. My passport was in the inside pocket of my jacket along with my wallet, and surely any thief would have taken the wallet, not the passport. It contained my own money, the school's money, and my credit cards. My passport would be no use to any pickpocket – unless he had the extremely good fortune to look exactly like me.

*****

As the coach lumbered off, I turned and headed for the town. I'd got enough money to take a train back north or to find a hotel for the night. I opted for the latter.

It was such a shame; up until that point, everything was going so well. On the coach, I'd instructed my two juniors at length about my rules for the visit and my expectations of them. I'd repeated everything in school many times before we left, but it never harms to reiterate. Ann and Mary were both in their 20s, and wholly dependent on my leadership. Now they'd be on their own with 30-odd pupils – I hadn't counted the exact number, but I'd told the pair of them to do it when we first boarded the coach and again after a brief stop at the motorway services. How they'd cope without my supervision, I dreaded to think.

On reflection, I think the proper thing would have been for the whole visit to be called off and for us to retrace our journey back to school. In my absence, any kind of disaster might be looming.

The seafront area near the port had several budget hostelries – Premier Inn, Travelodge, that sort of thing – and I asked a passer-by whether he could direct me to 5-star accommodation. He looked at me as if I was mad – I doubt he even understood the term '5-star.' I eventually found an establishment claiming 4 stars a short distance from the seafront and booked in, reluctantly accepting that this was the best on offer.

Once in my room, I took some executive decisions. Of course, my first thought was for the reputation of the school, so I sent my colleagues a message:

> Good afternoon. Kindly keep me informed of progress of visit. ON NO ACCOUNT repeat NO ACCOUNT attempt to communicate with school directly. All communication MUST be directed through me. Peter

I decided not to take an early train home. If I was spotted arriving in town, people would wonder what had happened and why I was back so early when we were scheduled to be in Normandy for nearly a week. They'd ask why I hadn't gone back to school to teach my classes; I didn't intend to, and I was determined to take advantage of the five full days I'd cancelled my lessons and Marjorie, our Deputy Head, had booked a supply teacher.

And so, I resolved my plan. I'd stay in Dover for the week, relax in the spring weather and enjoy some leisure time, then rejoin my group as it returned from France for the journey north. But in messages to school, I'd imply I was on the continent with them, directing matters as only I knew how.

I checked into the hotel dining room for lunch. In my confusion as I left the coach, I'd forgotten to collect the packed meal which my cleaner, Mrs Lee, had prepared for me. Pupils had been instructed to bring food for the journey, as we knew we wouldn't be at our hotel in Rouen until late afternoon.

I ordered a prawn salad, followed by trifle. Then I noticed the cheese trolley, so I helped myself a couple of times from that. To finish, I was going to order a cup of tea, but I remembered the French prefer coffee – I was still wearing my 'Frenchman's outfit,' to which I'd added the beret – so I sent the waitress for a *demitasse*. I had to explain to her what that was.

In the afternoon I went for a walk. It was a sunny day, and most pleasant to stroll round the shops and cafés of the seaside town. I bought a few glossy magazines to read in the evening, in case there wasn't anything good on television. The rest of my group, which by now would be motoring across northern France, had pretty much slipped my mind. I did have one concern, though: how would I get the bill for my hotel, plus a week's meals in and around Dover, past the bursar as expenses? Having worked very hard to organise the visit, I was determined I shouldn't be out of pocket. I'd unselfishly chosen a modest 4-star hotel, not a 5-star one, and I wasn't proposing to dine on champagne and caviar every night! Having said that, nor was I prepared to compromise my high standards, and I anticipated visiting some of Dover's finer restaurants.

Back at my hotel, I was settling in at the bar with a pre-dinner Pernod and blackcurrant – a very French choice! – when my phone beeped. It was a text from my colleagues:

> Hi Peter. Just arrived in Rouen. Can you tell us name of hotel? Driver unable to find it. Mary

When I say I'd worked very hard to organise the visit, I don't mean I'd done every little thing myself. We used a travel agency which specialises in school tours, and I'd let my two junior colleagues deal with them. We'd also collected in money from the pupils: I'd given strict instructions to the bursar on exactly how to do that, and several reminders to count it carefully and keep a record of how much each pupil had paid. I let my subordinates send letters to the parents telling them what their children should bring with them – a task best done by a woman, I felt. My cleaner, Mrs Lee, had packed my suitcase, making sure that all my clothes were properly washed and ironed beforehand.

So, naturally, I didn't know the name of the hotel. Fancy them messaging me to ask! I composed an authoritative reply:

> Find name and address of hotel by contacting travel agent. You have their details. If not look on internet. Peter

I leaned back with my Pernod, confident in the
knowledge that I'd once again ridden to the rescue.
My phone pinged again:

OK will do. But it's 7:00 pm so travel agent
might be closed by now. PS We found your
passport. It had slipped down beside your
seat. Do you want us to send it to you at
school? Mary

Well, how annoying! I knew I'd been right all
along – of course I hadn't come away without my
passport.

I sent another text, this time to the headmaster,
Mr Bryant – a pompous old windbag who loves the
sound of his own voice, even when he has nothing
worth saying. He was in favour of us bringing pupils
to France, and I told him how much hard work I'd
done to organise everything alongside teaching my
classes and my responsibilities as Head of Subject.

Bonsoir Directeur Bryant! Greetings
from Rouen! Arrived here safely and are
now settled into our luxuriously appointed
hotel. All smiles on faces of lucky children!
Off to dinner now, exploring Rouen
tomorrow. Kind regards, Peter

I enjoyed my dinner of Dover sole. An impromptu
witticism occurred to me, with which I was able to
delight the waitress, asking if it was served with
Dover potatoes and Dover peas. I bet she'd never
heard that one before! I re-read my text to Mr

Bryant, and thought, "That'll keep the old fool happy!"

With hindsight, I'm not fully sure that was the case.

*****

After a night reflecting on my masterful handling of the passport crisis, I woke on Tuesday refreshed and ready for another day in Dover. My striped jersey had served its purpose, so I selected another Pierre Cardin top that was equally *décontracté*. I kept the slacks, though – my Gallic disguise still had work to do.

The hotel served a full English breakfast, including kedgeree, which I'd heard of but never tried before. An odd mixture, a curried fish risotto is the best way I can describe it. Not what a man wants first thing in the morning, so I sent it back and ordered the old stand-by of bacon, mushrooms, sausages, black pudding, baked beans, tomatoes, fried eggs and toast instead.

It's ironic that I've never been to France, despite speaking the language superbly. Of course, that's not something I share with my colleagues or pupils; I naturally let them assume I'm a regular visitor to French shores. France is hyped up, in my view: over-priced restaurants, especially if you stumble on one of those *nouvelle cuisine* establishments with their tiny, undercooked portions and surly staff who don't treat customers with the respect they deserve.

It's not hard to show a knowledge of France, though. The glossy magazines print enough photographs of Paris for me to feel I know the place intimately, and thanks to the *Daily Mail* travel writers, I can refer to its restaurants and other attractions whenever I need. Also, although I'm not a fan of modern French cinema, there is one film I show my pupils as often as I can: Friday afternoons, last lesson before half-term, that kind of thing. It's called *Amélie*, and it's set in Paris. The English subtitles make it easy for the children to follow – I don't need them myself, of course – and it gives such a complete picture of life in France that one doesn't feel any need to go there and learn more. Not everyone appreciates *Amélie* as much as I do: I sometimes spot my pupils rolling their eyes and muttering, "Oh no, not that again," as I set up the DVD player. I stamp down on such insubordination immediately, of course.

One thing I do ask myself is this: thousands of people try to migrate from France to the south coast of England every year. It may even be tens of thousands – no-one publishes accurate figures. But why? France is a respectable country, despite its obvious shortcomings in the hospitality industry. People have jobs and earn decent wages. Some of the women are quite attractive, despite not shaving their armpits and other areas. Why, then, do so many Frenchmen load themselves into tiny rubber dinghies and try to cross the Channel to England?

I decided that on my first morning in Dover, I'd head down towards the beaches where many of these landings must take place. With the spring weather and calmer seas, crossings must become less hazardous. Perhaps I might meet some French immigrants coming ashore and ask them – in French of course – why they find England so attractive and want to leave France so urgently. They'd be delighted to find such a fluent French speaker to greet them, and they might even give me the answers that the British press fails to provide. I jotted down some questions I might put to them:

- *Pardon, monsieur, avez-vous un agréable voyage?*
- *Pourquoi visitez-vous l'Angleterre?*
- *Préférez-vous l'Angleterre ou la France? Parlez-moi pourquoi.*

I hadn't walked far when I met a cluster of policemen. A demonstration was taking place further along the esplanade. I could see a BBC van, cameras and a reporter with a microphone. I asked the police whether it was possible to go any further and they said yes, but not to engage with the marchers, as they would arrest anyone who went beyond the bounds of 'peaceful protest.'

A little further along, the reporter and his cameraman were filming what appeared to be interviews with members of the public.

Now, I'm very accomplished in front of the camera. Our school's Media Studies department recently filmed a series of interviews with the more important members of staff, as well as the most popular ones. I think I'm unique in fitting into both categories! From that, and from pictures of myself on my walls at home, I know that my left is my 'best side,' as the professionals call it. To show one's 'left profile,' as it's also known in the business, one should look to the right of the camera. Never look directly into the lens; eye contact with the viewer breaks the illusion of natural performance. You'll find that's true for films as well as TV programmes, once you know to look for it.

I'm normally very annoyed by interviews with common people on local news bulletins. They seem to pick the most ignorant, self-opinionated numpties and televise their views as if they're the Gospel. For example, if there's a news item relating to schools, they always allow parents to appear on screen: "What do you think of the teachers' strike?" they'll ask. As if parents would know the hard work that teachers do, the hours they put in, the marking, the after-school meetings. Of course they've got nothing worth saying, even though they usually shout it loudly enough!

I pushed my way to the front where a producer was trying to find willing interviewees. I eagerly volunteered—a memorable appearance now might lead to television stardom!

"What do you think about today's protests?" the reporter asked.

"Today's protests?" I replied, presenting my left profile to the camera. "Well, I believe in human rights. Everyone has the right to express an opinion."

"But are you in favour of third world migrants entering the UK by these illegal crossings?"

"Certainly not," I said decisively. "These people are French. They have other perfectly good options—the ferry, Eurotunnel, or by air—all much safer than rubber dinghies." In saying this, I struck a distinguished pose, imagining myself as Winston Churchill gazing out across the Channel.

The assistant thanked me for my contribution, adding that it might feature on local news or even make the nationals. I rather hoped that too—fancy me appearing on national TV!

*****

Feeling quite elated – a TV celebrity, though no-one would recognise me yet – I had a further look round the town, then went into a cosy-looking café for some lunch. I ordered a lobster salad, made with locally caught lobsters, according to the menu. A glass of wine too, to celebrate my screen appearance – a large *Pinot Grigio*. If the bursar was paying, I was going to enjoy myself!

I was still eating when my phone pinged — another message from my team:

> Hi Peter, we survived our first night in France. Fortunately, a kind and very good-looking policeman helped us find somewhere to stay. Now on the loose in Rouen! Regards, Mary

On the loose, indeed! I hoped no-one was taking advantage of the lack of discipline which my absence might encourage. I texted back:

> Lucky that you found a *gendarme* who spoke English. Ensure all are behaving themselves. Peter

I couldn't imagine any junior having my ability to engage with the local police in French, and it seemed worthwhile to remind them of the fact. After all, there's a good reason I'm their superior. Two minutes later I had a reply:

> He was an *agent de police*, not a *gendarme*. Spoke only French – no English. Extremely handsome, though! Accommodation not the best but should do better tonight. We were in police cells. Frightening! Mary

That's twice they'd mentioned the policeman's good looks. They never say anything like that about me! I didn't read all the next bit, but hopefully 'better tonight' would mean finding the hotel which the travel agent had promised us.

I spent the evening in my hotel and had another excellent meal. I was relaxing in the bar, waiting for the 10 o'clock news and looking forward to my possible TV appearance, when my phone rang.

"Is that Peter? Sebastian Bryant here."

I recognised his pompous old voice. The silly fool is the headmaster, though, so I responded appropriately.

"Why good evening, Headmaster, thank you so much for calling. How can I help you?"

"Peter, I've just seen the early evening news. Aren't you supposed to be in France?"

"Why yes, Headmaster," I reassured him, "I'm with the rest of my group."

"Are you sure?" he asked, "I've just seen you on the BBC – a vox-pop interview in Dover."

"Oh no," I assuaged, "That wasn't me. That was a lookalike, a Frenchman, he looks like me, but I've never met him."

"Peter," he said sharply, "If you've never met him, how do you know what he looks like? Tell me honestly, are you in France right now, or still in Dover?"

"I'm in France," I said. "I'm with the school party. I'm the party leader, I hasten to remind you. We've just been for dinner and the pupils are about to go to their rooms."

"So where did you have dinner?" he barked. "And can you tell me the name of your hotel?"

"We ate in our hotel," I said. Thank goodness for my lightning-fast thinking! "Give me a minute, I'll just go outside and read you the name of it."

Fortunately, he didn't take me up on my offer. "Peter," he insisted, "You're not in France. Please tell me exactly what's going on."

I thought that was insolent. The man was virtually accusing me of lying! I terminated the call, saying that interference over the Channel was causing the signal to break up.

My TV appearance made the national news. It wasn't the first item, which was about the royal family, but there was footage of the demonstration mixed in with archive pictures of people climbing out of small rubber boats on beaches. Mine was one of two interviews featured – I suppose they had to make it clear that not everyone has such well-informed opinions as I do. With all the noise in the hotel bar, not everyone was able to hear me, but they must have been struck by how I presented my left profile to the camera – even without the words, I looked decisive and debonair. And no doubt in homes up and down the country people would be giving their full attention to what I had to say. Perhaps I'll be invited to appear on *Question Time* or *Newsnight* if either of those programmes are still running!

*****

Wednesday morning brought more blue skies and another irritating text from my juniors.

> Hi Peter. Hotel in *rue Cauchoise* near town centre. Fun time last night! Bar open till late and the girls made a big hit with the locals. Mary is a bit hung over now, but we should get out around lunchtime. Regards, Ann

So that's alright – they've found the hotel. I didn't read the rest. It annoys me when people give me *War and Peace*; I wish they'd just get to the point.

There isn't much to see in Dover: a castle, which is quite old, and some secret tunnels which aren't secret at all. You just follow the signs, join a queue, and buy a ticket. Of course, I had to visit the famous White Cliffs – a short taxi-ride out of town, but there's a tearoom, and some quite nice views if you like looking out of windows.

That evening, I thought I'd better send word back to school. A message would do; I didn't want to get into another debate with pompous old Bryant. First, I texted Ann and Mary:

> URGENT.   Report progress of visit IMMEDIATELY. List activities for today AND TOMORROW. Peter

I was angry that they took a full ten minutes to respond – the whole time it took me to drink my

Pernod and blackcurrant in the hotel bar. Then a reply popped up in my inbox:

> Hello Peter, and a pleasant evening to you too. Flaubert this morning – museum, cathedral (you must know the scene with Emma and Léon) then in afternoon *Le Gros Horloge, La Vieille Ville* and *La Place du Marché* where Joan of Arc was burned at the stake. Also visited *Palais de Justice* where Pierre Corneille worked – did you know what his second job was? Hotel was raided by police – the joint was a real *Maison Tellier*. Might try Novotel tonight. Tomorrow is cheese farm – *vive le Camembert*! And Calvados distillery. Yum yum! *Bons baisers*! Mary

I skimmed this message, but it didn't make sense. What was a Flaubert, I wondered. My pocket dictionary didn't help. I assumed Emma and Léon were two people, but not two of our pupils so far as I knew, so I wondered why they were telling me this. Then there was a fat something, so I turned to my pocket dictionary again. *Horloge* means clock (of course, I know the word *pendule*, it's the word we teach our pupils), but with my eagle eye I spotted something amiss: in the dictionary, it's *une horloge*, feminine, so *le Gros Horloge* is wrong. I dashed off a quick message to point out their error – not as though I want to vaunt my superior knowledge, of course – before sending my report to the headmaster:

Bonsoir from France! Another exciting day superbly organised by me. This morning, we visited a Flaubert (very interesting, most pupils had never seen one before). In the afternoon we saw *La Grosse Horloge* and the Market Square and Old Town, where we saw Pierre Corneille at work. Plans for tomorrow include tasting local *fromage* and *baisers*. Pupils beside themselves with anticipation! Peter

You'll notice I cleverly alluded to *Flaubert* and *baisers* without saying what they were. I also translated Old Town and Market Square into English for Mr Bryant's benefit, since I'm sure he doesn't speak a word of French, and I corrected my juniors' error with the gender of *une horloge*. It proves I know these things even if they don't!

Pompous old Bryant soon replied. Honestly, it's high time he retired. Here's what he wrote.

Peter! I said last night I didn't believe you were in France, and I still don't. FYI, Rouen's *Gros Horloge* acquired masculine gender well before the 1700s when *horloge* became feminine. Do you know who Flaubert was? Clue: he was a 19th Century French novelist. I also suspect you don't know what Pierre Corneille's first job was, never mind his second. Further clue: he was a playwright who wrote neo-classical French tragedies. I very much doubt you

saw him at work today; he died in 1684.
You've not been to a *Maison Tellier*, and I
suspect you've never tasted *baisers* either.
The two may be connected. We need to talk
– I'll catch up with you in school on
Monday. Regards, SB

Claims he'll catch up with me! Well, that won't
happen – I'm far too quick witted for him.

I didn't eat in my hotel every night, or every
lunchtime. In my Frenchman's guise, I visited
different restaurants of varying qualities. I was
quite critical on occasion, and sometimes told the
staff just how much better things are in a French
estaminet. Even though France is just over 20 miles
away, and you can see it on a clear day, very few
waiters had any notion of the French language, and
certainly none to the degree that I can boast.

On Saturday, I went to meet my group when it
landed – actually, they were early, as they'd given
me the wrong arrival time. They'd said midday. But
I know all about *le décollage* – that's the time
difference between Britain and France – so I got to
the port at around twenty past one. Apparently
'midday' was the time when they'd been ready to
continue their journey. Claiming they'd been
waiting over an hour, some of the pupils were cheeky
enough to look pointedly at their watches and tut. I
wasn't going to stand for that! I drew myself up to
my full height, and announced, "As Head of
Department and Party Leader, it is my prerogative

to start an activity at whatever time I choose. If that means the rest of you have to wait, then so be it."

That told them! There was no more muttering after that.

Of course, I was magnanimous in victory. Once the coach was underway, I sauntered between the seats and graciously asked some of the more presentable looking pupils how their visit had been.

"It was great, sir," they said. "France is brill."

"Yes, all thanks to my planning and organisation," I pointed out.

"Miss White and Miss Flowers are tops," others insisted.

"What about the awful accommodation?" I subtly enquired, trying not to put words into their mouths, of course.

"Great hotel," they said. "Food was fantastic, too!"

This wasn't what I'd been led to believe. "And nothing to do, except look at a boring cheese factory and a dreary museum," I hinted.

"Sir, no way!" they argued. "We made our own cheese, and we made some apple beer. Joan of Arc was a legend, and the people who showed us around were ace."

"What? Who showed you around?" I demanded to know. I'd heard nothing of this. Perhaps it was Pierre Corneille, or maybe Emma and Léon.

"Our friends from the French school," they told me. "We learned some great new words."

From the way they giggled, I suspected those words might not be suitable for their GCSE exams, which were coming up quite soon.

"We want to do French in the sixth form," they clamoured, "Do you think Miss White and Miss Flowers could be our teachers?"

This was plainly both insulting and ridiculous. I've always taught the top sets and the sixth form; that's been my decision ever since I was appointed to the school as Head of Subject. I went back to my seat behind the driver where I sat down and pretended to fall asleep.

I must have fallen asleep for real, because when I woke up, we were nearly home. I phoned for a taxi to pick me up at school, and it was waiting for me when we arrived. I instructed Ann and Mary to deal with the parents and make sure every child was safely off the premises before they left.

The following Monday, miserable old Bryant was less grateful than he ought to have been for all my efforts. Fortunately, he'd stopped arguing about whether I'd been to France or not, but he thought Ann and Mary had done the right thing regarding my passport. They hadn't done anything at all! They'd offered to post it home, I'd not insisted, and now it was on Mr Bryant's desk for me to collect.

Had I not worried about the children spending the first night in police cells and the second in a brothel, Bryant asked me. I said that was news to me; our accommodation was first-rate, as I'd told him in my messages. He said he knew it was, but was I aware that Ann and Mary had been playing a little joke on me by telling me the opposite? It then transpired that they'd gone behind my back and told Bryant they'd invented lies – yes, lies – to irritate me. And this had been going on from the start.

"And the handsome policeman they told me about – they mentioned him twice – am I to presume he didn't exist?" Mr Bryant didn't answer that; he merely laughed.

"Bad news about Joan of Arc too," he intimated, "If you'll pardon my French."

"What do you mean?" I snapped back at him.

"*Elle a été cuite sans jamais avoir été crue*," he sniggered, in the most childish way possible for a grown man.

"I'm glad you find that amusing," I sneered, "Because I certainly don't."

"Ask one of the others," he offered, "They'll explain it for you."

I'm not going to ask them. I'm the Head of Department, and I know best. They'll do as I say.

I'm also far better looking than any French *gendarme*, imaginary or not, especially from the left profile.

THE INSPECTORS AND I

I received a text message from the headmaster's secretary one Thursday evening.

To: Peter Trumper (PT)

Please note there will be an emergency staff meeting at morning break tomorrow (Friday) in the staffroom. Your attendance shall be required.

PP Sebastian Bryant (SB) Headmaster

Speculation was rife as we arrived in school the following morning. Either the school was in financial difficulties, which would mean redundancies among the lower ranks and a few early retirements for the senior staff, or else we were due an inspection by Ofsted – the government's police force for schools – in the next few days.

Well before break, everybody knew what was coming. The bursar had let slip that the school was financially sound and there were no threats to our jobs. Ofsted it was to be.

Mr Bryant, the headmaster, confirmed as much, but in his usual long-winded way, as if he expected us to be surprised by what he was announcing. I felt as if I'd known it for weeks.

Bryant reminded us how it would work. Ofsted inspections always start on a Monday and last one week. Informing the school on Thursday evening allows time for last-minute planning on Friday and over the weekend. He continued at some length, but I didn't need to listen. My department is always well prepared. My own classes are superb, of course, and I make a point of scrutinising my juniors on a regular basis. I watch their lessons, and I tell them quite bluntly what I dislike about them. When I submit my reports, I always add a few extra criticisms just to emphasise how much better my teaching is than theirs.

I therefore had no worries when I arrived at school on Monday morning. By lunchtime, I still hadn't seen an inspector, although one or two other teachers had. The head of Drama, 'Luvvie' Laithwaite, had spotted some, and he demonstrated what he called the 'inspector's walk.' "It's halfway between strutting about as though they own the place and trying to be inconspicuous because they know they're unwelcome," he explained. "Like a Tory MP visiting his constituency." I liked that line – in fact, I used it myself several times.

At lunchtime, I was striding down the corridor to get a cup of coffee from the canteen. Coffee is free to staff, and we can push in at the front of the queue. Suddenly, from the meeting room, a squat, bulky figure emerged who probably had the same intention as I did. We almost collided – it was as well I wasn't heading back to the staffroom with my coffee in one hand and a cream doughnut in the other.

I transfixed him with my withering sneer, and was just about to growl, "And where do you think you're going, young man?" I often say that to pupils who are not where they ought to be.

Just in time, I realised he wasn't a pupil, but nor did I recognise him as another teacher. As I tried to place him, he looked at me in surprise, and exclaimed, "Well, if it isn't Peter!"

I thought for a moment he was going to hug me, but he must have sensed my unease and instead thrust his arm out towards me. I shook hands with him and introduced myself: "Mister Peter Trumper, HOD. Head of Department, Modern Languages. *Enchanté, monsieur!*" I have a very firm, manly handshake but the vigour of his pumping fist nearly lifted me off the floor.

"Peter, Peter," he repeated, "Don't you remember me?   Rotherham Technical Institute, Teacher Training Course! I'm George Roland."

No-one at school knows where I qualified. I always imply that I studied at Oxford; I therefore didn't want it blurted out that my only diploma comes from a much less prestigious institution. I tried to manoeuvre us both into the meeting room, away from public view, but he blocked my way.

"Can't go in there," he insisted, "Too much confidential material."

I studied his face and finally placed him, even though it was over fifteen years since we'd last met.

"George Roland," I declared, "I remember you now. Roly Poly Roland! But didn't you fail the course? The only one of us not to pass, if I'm correct. Something to do with sleeping with a pupil during teaching practice!"

Now he was the one pulling me into the meeting room. Although happy to blurt out my credentials, he certainly didn't want his own indiscretions exposed.

"Three pupils, actually," he grunted, without any hint of shame, "But nothing was ever proved."

The meeting room was, as he'd indicated, filled with documents and files. It had been given over to the inspectors, several of whom had brought laptops and other similar devices. No-one was in the room; apart from Roly Poly himself, they must all have been spread throughout the school as they went about their inquisitorial business.

"You must be one of the inspectors, then," I deduced.

"Lead Inspector," he replied. "I call the team together, delegate tasks, then write the report at the end of the week."

"That sounds terribly important," I schmoozed. If George Roland was now so influential, a little flattery might not go amiss. I could have added that he'd put on weight; the roly-poliness that I remembered had given way to outright obesity. My weight plus half as much again, I'd guess, even though he was a good four inches shorter than me. And he hadn't aged as well: I still pass as early thirties; he, on the other hand, was quite obviously the wrong side of forty.

"Peter," he said, lowering his voice in a conspiratorial sort of way, "We must get together. What about dinner tonight? On me, of course. You're the local man. Where would you recommend?"

"Aren't you eating in your hotel?" I asked. "I assume you're all staying locally?"

"We're at the Imperial," he replied, "But we don't want to eat there. Too many ears! We need to catch up on old times! Somewhere out of town, maybe?"

I thought of an upmarket little Italian restaurant in one of the outlying villages. It made sense for me to drive – I'm not only an outstandingly good driver, but I'd also taken recent delivery of a brand-new BMW convertible, a top-of-the-range model with leather seats and all the optional extras. I promised to pick him up at his hotel at 7:00, having reserved a table for 7:30.

That afternoon, none of my lessons was visited by an inspector. A pity, I thought, since my best lessons are usually on a Monday. I've had all weekend to prepare, and I've noted down two or three clever retorts which I can use if a pupil makes a mistake in class or scores a low mark in a test. Later in the week, I might not always remember which of my spontaneous witticisms I've shared with a particular group, so I sometimes either miss an opportunity or end up repeating something I've already said to the same class.

So, that evening I was leaving my house at a quarter to seven. My neighbour Mr Laurels was putting his car into his garage, and he commented that it was rare to see me going out on a weekday night. He also observed that although stylish as always, I was quite casually dressed. It was true: I had on a blazer, an open necked shirt, smart chinos and a pair of loafers. I wasn't going to a parents' evening at school, he surmised, where I'd normally wear one of my more formal lounge suits with a jaunty tie. The sound of our conversation drew Mrs Snoop from next-door-but-one, who inferred that I must have a date and wanted to pry into who it might be.

"Is it another teacher?" she enquired.

I like to be discreet about my private life, whilst hinting that it's more adventurous that it is, so I said I was seeing an esteemed young member of the legal profession and was taking her out to dinner.

"Where did you meet her?" the interfering old crone demanded to know. I couldn't say I met her in court – she'd wonder what I'd been getting up to – so I said we'd met at a party.

"But you never go to any parties," she said. "If you did, I'd have noticed you leaving your house."

Rather than be drawn into a conversation I didn't want to pursue, I said I had to rush as my date would be waiting for me. "Yes, you know what it is with these women who solicit," Laurels interjected. "Time is money!"

I didn't appreciate the insinuation, but I chose to ignore it and slammed the car door heavily.

That evening, then, I drove Roly Poly Roland to *La Dolce Vita* in Westhorpe, a village about twenty minutes away on the road towards the moors. I'd been there once before, so I knew we'd be well fed, and they have an impressive wine cellar, although as driver I'd be restricted to a single glass of *Pinot Grigio*. On the way, I naturally wanted to tell him about my importance as head of subject and the excellence of my lessons, so that he'd be well prepared if he or a colleague should attend one of my classes. But first, I asked him how the inspections were going, noting that I personally hadn't seen an inspector apart from him.

Roly Poly explained that inspectors usually spend Monday mornings scrutinising documents in the school they're visiting, looking for evidence of poor exam results, disciplinary problems, or other examples of mismanagement. They watch lessons on Monday afternoon, all day Tuesday and on Wednesday morning. On Wednesday afternoon they discuss their findings, and on Thursday morning they write their reports. After lunch, the inspectors head for home: it can be quite a long drive as they're often drafted in from all over the country.

"And when can I anticipate being inspected?" I asked.

"You won't be this time," he revealed. "Fact is, we haven't got an inspector in the team who can speak a foreign language. And I do have a conscience. I wouldn't make one of my men visit a lesson where he had no idea about what he was seeing. I've done some bad things in my time, but that's not one of them."

"The other inspectors are all experts, then?" It seemed a reasonable guess.

"Up to a point. They'll have GCSE, maybe even A-Level. Enough to understand the content, especially in lower school."

By now we'd arrived at the restaurant. I parked, revving the engine to make sure of being noticed, and we went inside. Immediately we were shown to a table, menus appeared, and we were offered drinks. Roly Poly had a beer; I asked for a sparkling mineral water, preferably a *Perrier*, knowing I would allow myself a glass of wine with the meal.

"That means we won't see you after Thursday?" I confirmed.

"Not necessarily," he said. "After my colleagues have written their reports, I paste them all together in the final statement. I usually spend Friday on that. I could go home and do it, or I could stay on here. Fact is, there's a very attractive barmaid in the Imperial, so once the others have gone, I'll have her all to myself, if you get my drift. But let's change the subject. What became of you after our year together at the Tech?"

I was delighted to tell him, and as our starters and then our main courses arrived, I described the high points of my distinguished career in several leading schools, taking care not to name them in case he followed them up. I never got my glass of *Pinot Grigio*; Roly Poly ordered a bottle of *Trebbiano d'Abruzzo* and I had a glass of that with my antipasti of *crostini* and main course of *vitello tonnato*.

"I don't remember languages being your thing at College," he said to me as we finished our main courses and studied the dessert menu. "Which language do you teach?"

"*Oh, le français, le français bien-sûr!*" I proclaimed. "*Mais je parle très très bien l'Allemagne et l'Italienne aussi.*" I said this a little louder and more dramatically than I needed to, and I was pleased to note that it drew me some admiring glances from diners at the surrounding tables.

"I didn't think Rotherham offered foreign languages," he said. "I don't remember anyone else who was training to teach French."

He was correct, so I explained how I'd enrolled on the TEFL course – that's Teaching English as a Foreign Language. My pupils had mostly been European au pairs and Asian taxi drivers.

"Ah yes, all the tasty foreign au pair girls," he mused. "Plenty of opportunity there to get your leg over, I'll bet. I'll tell you what – if you speak the lingo, try ordering our desserts in Italian. I'll have zabaglione, but don't you be influenced by me."

The waitress arrived to take our order. "*Una zabaglione*," I confidently commanded, "*Y para mi, una gelata por favor.*"

"*Uno zabaione e un gelato*," she repeated, although her pronunciation was no match for mine. "*Che gusto di gelato per favore?*"

"*Si si si!*" I replied, with a touch of irritation. "*Che gusto el gelata.*"

Since I'd ordered ice cream, it shouldn't have been beyond the poor girl's intelligence to realise that I enjoy ice cream.

"No, no, *che gusto* means what flavour," she claimed.

I ignored her impertinence. "*Ah, naturalmente*," I said, and I tried to think of a flavour in Italian. "*Io prendo vanilla y chocolata.*"

"*Vaniglia e cioccolato*," she repeated. I don't know whether the silly young thing was deaf or if she thought I might change my mind. But Roly Poly seemed suitably impressed, and I was pleased to have had the chance to show off my prowess.

I'd still got half of my glass of wine, but I noticed that Roly Poly had finished the rest of the bottle. He noticed it too, and he called the waitress back.

"And a half bottle of dessert wine," he ordered, making no effort to address her in Italian. She brought the wine ahead of the desserts. "*Gracias, señorita*," I told her on his behalf, and she smiled, no doubt overwhelmed by my mastery of the language.

"So, Peter, if you started out in TEFL," he asked, "what got you into European languages? Didn't your father's company have a job for you – everyone in town knew about Trumper's tits."

I rose above his vulgar put-down. "My natural ability," I modestly replied. "Also, when I was teaching TEFL, I noticed my classes weren't making much progress. I thought: 'I can speak their languages far better than they can speak mine'." That only applied to the Europeans, I added; I had no interest in acquiring any Arabic or Asian languages.

My father did indeed own a company, and a very successful one. He sold it when he retired, and generously shared the proceeds with me. My brand-new BMW was paid for with part of that windfall. The company was called Trumper's IT Solutions, which explains why, until it was pointed out to him, he sent his technicians out with TITS emblazoned on their overalls, as Roly Poly had reminded me. The Tech had a big IT upgrade just before I was there, and Trumper's had installed new, networked computers throughout the campus. Some said my place on the course had been awarded in exchange for a reduction on the bill, an opinion which Roly Poly apparently still shared, but I know that's just jealousy.

His banter aside, I quite enjoyed Roly Poly's company. Not just because he was paying for the meal; he asked questions and seemed a good listener. I felt moved to return the favour by asking him about his own career.

"I'm truly a self-made man," he claimed as our desserts arrived and we started to eat again. "I left school at 18 – no great shakes at A Level, and I went to work at the Town Hall. Finance Department – why they put me there, I've no idea. It certainly wasn't my Maths! By the time I was 21, I'd done it all, risen to the top, I needed a new challenge. Someone suggested teaching."

"Which was where we met," I pointed out. "So, if I was English for Foreigners, what was your specialism?"

"Primary teaching," he told me. "Fact is, you don't need A-Level to teach the under-elevens, and men in primary schools are as rare as hens' teeth! They promised me I'd be a headmaster by the time I was thirty."

"Ah, but then you failed the certificate," I pointed out. That triggered an unpleasant thought and, tactfully of course, I checked my facts with him, "You'd been caught sleeping with pupils – three of them, you said. They weren't primary school children, were they?"

"Heavens, no!" he reassured me, "What do you take me for? Do you remember, in the first term we all did a day a week in a secondary school? Well, that was where it happened."

"But that must be why you failed. And yet, a lot of teachers do get away with that kind of thing."

"No, you're wrong there, lad. Nothing was ever proven. Besides, I didn't fail – I may have had poor marks for planning, organisation, punctuality, lesson reviews, not marking the kids' work, you know, technical things like that, but I got a certificate of attendance. I've still got the document at home to prove it. They told me I wouldn't get a reference if I applied for a teaching job, but that's all."

"So..... you weren't going to be a primary school head before you were thirty," I reiterated. "I was a head of department when I was still in my late twenties." That was an exaggeration, but I knew he couldn't prove it. "What did you do instead?" I asked him.

"I went back to the Town Hall," he continued, "And soon after that, I got a similar position down south. County Education Department, this time. I sailed through the interview, made a great play about my teaching experience, and I was in."

"But you didn't have any teaching experience!" I exclaimed.

"They weren't to know that. Remember, it was down south – a long way from Rotherham! So, I quickly made a name for myself in education. We introduced quality control – actually, it was my idea – and we started inspecting our own schools. If you're confident, it's not hard to look like you know what you're doing. Especially if you're from the council."

"That's true," I affirmed, "It's remarkable how people always trust an expert."

"And then," he continued, after briefly acknowledging the compliment, "several other counties bought in to the programme – my programme, that is. Eventually, Ofsted muscled in and took over school inspections. Well, some said a vast, central-government-sponsored bureaucracy would mean the end of us County Hall mandarins, but I had other ideas. I suggested we should offer 'pre-Ofsted' checks – and that became a big money-spinner too."

"A pre-Ofsted inspection?" I queried, "You'd think Ofsted alone would be frightening enough to most schools."

"Exactly," Roly Poly replied, "So we said – and this was why my idea was so brilliant, of course – that we'd visit schools who were due an Ofsted inspection, charge them a fee, and tell them where they were going wrong. Tell them what they needed to fix before Ofsted arrived and closed them down. Never mind a nice little earner! Fact is, it was a fucking goldmine! Schools were so shit-scared of Ofsted, they'd do anything to soften the blow."

"But then you transferred to Ofsted yourself," I prompted.

"Yes, I was head-hunted," he confirmed, "But I still work full-time at County Hall. I get time off to do inspections, then when I'm not out and about, I'm back at my desk. Best of both worlds – paid holiday and still on full pay back at the ranch!"

"Impressive," I agreed. I noticed he had his eye on another table where a young couple had just paid their bill and left. As the waitress came over to clear away the plates and glasses, he clicked his fingers to draw her attention.

"Excuse me, love," he called out, "Could I have that bill that's been left behind? You'd only throw it away, wouldn't you?" The waitress picked it up, checked that it had indeed been paid, and passed it to him, no doubt thinking like me that it was a strange request.

Roly Poly must have seen my quizzical expression. "You're wondering why I want this, aren't you?" he asked. I nodded, and he explained, "You see, our meal tonight, I'll put it through on Ofsted expenses. But I can put this bill in too, and make a few quid on it."

"Surely Ofsted won't believe you ate two meals in the same restaurant on the same evening?" I quizzed.

"Ofsted, no, but this one –" he waved the other couple's bill at me – "this one can go to my publishers. I'll tell them I was entertaining a teacher who's writing some lesson materials for us. I know just the person, and I believe he lives round these parts."

It sounded like a fraud to me, although I suppose when you travel for work then you can get away with these things. I hope I didn't sound like I was trying to ride the gravy train too, because I asked him how I might become an Ofsted inspector myself.

"Actually, I think I'd be rather good at it," I added.

"I'm sure you would," he agreed. "Fact is, there's not a lot to it. You visit a school, watch a few lessons, you form an opinion, and you give them a grade – one, two, three or four."

"Could I join Ofsted, then?" I asked. "How do you apply?"

"You couldn't," he told me. "You have to guarantee a minimum of ten weeks a year. That means there's no room for classroom teachers – you wouldn't get that much leave of absence. The only teachers that work for us are deputy heads who do nothing, and head teachers with a deputy who does everything."

"That's a shame," I said. "I'd have rather enjoyed it. Visiting a school and being able to stride around as though you own the place, you must feel like a Tory MP visiting his constituency." I was proud of that comparison, and I'm sure I told it even better than 'Luvvie' Laithwaite. "But what happens if the headteacher disagrees with your grade?"

"Then he's wrong, simple as that," Roly Poly replied. "You might think that's unfair, especially since we only see a fraction of what goes on in a school, but our word is the law."

"But once you've decided on a mark out of four, you still have to write the report that goes with it?"

"Again, that's quite easy," Roly Poly explained. "We have a list of stock phrases, so we choose the best ones and paste them together. Of course, I'm the author of the phrasebook – it's all my work. We avoid anything which might have legal repercussions. For example, we'd never say, 'This school's lessons are all a load of crap,' even if that's what we think. Instead, we say, 'We did not see sufficient lessons of high quality.' That gets us off the hook – the school may have very good classes, but they weren't the ones we happened to drop in on."

"I know you said we wouldn't be inspected in Languages," I reminded him, "But could you just poke your head round my classroom door for a moment? Then you could write in your report something like 'Mr Trumper's lessons are wonderful, and so much better than Mr Simpson's.' Which would be true, of course."

"Sorry," he conceded, "but that's another rule. We're not allowed to name names. The Teachers' Union forced that one on us."

"That's a shame," I said.

"Ah, but we soon found a way of turning the tables," he went on, triumph creeping back into his voice. "We might say, 'We saw two satisfactory lessons and six poor lessons.' Then we know that for weeks afterwards the teachers are arguing among themselves about whose lessons were any good and whose weren't, the poor bastards!"

"You can't give me an honourable mention, then?" I pleaded.

"Well, we can imply things," he hinted, tapping the side of his nose and winking in a knowing way. "And I might just do that. Fact is, Peter, you know things about me that others don't. Those schoolgirls. No smoke without fire. So, here's my offer. You don't let on that we know each other, and I put something in the report like 'The inspectors noted excellent management in the French Department.' Like I said, no names mentioned, but it's obvious who we're referring to. Do we have a deal?"

It sounded very fair to me. Roly Poly wanted to celebrate with a brandy, but I declined, knowing I'd already had a glass of wine and still had to drive first to his hotel and then back to my house.

"Well look, you get off home," he suggested, "and I'll hang on here for a couple more drinks. Fact is, I'm going to have a crack at one of the waitresses – her in the short skirt and the fishnets." As he spoke, the girl in question headed across to our table to clear away our dessert bowls and glasses. "We'll either go back to her place, or we'll take a taxi from here to my hotel," he resumed, once she was out of earshot.

Roly Poly had already drunk considerably more than me, and I was sober enough to foresee a problem. Even if the waitress succumbed to his charms, he'd have to wait until she finished serving, and after that she'd probably have to help tidying and clearing everything away. It might be late before she finished her shift, and then he'd have to allow time for a taxi to drive out from town. I offered again to run him back to the Imperial, but he was adamant, and his only request was that I pass him the discarded bill from another nearby table on my way out.

"I've got a number of projects, and they all look after me for expenses," he explained.

I didn't see Roly Poly again for the duration of the inspectors' visit, which was perhaps as well since we'd agreed we wouldn't acknowledge one another in school. Had he managed to have his way with the young waitress? If I'd asked him, I'm sure he'd have lied about it, as he probably had about so much of his glittering career.

He'd slipped my mind by Wednesday afternoon when, to celebrate the end of the inspection, I was just about to show my class the French film *Amélie*. It's a marvellous film which I've shown them many times, although there are some scenes where you need to fast-forward because the content is a bit racy. Very French, I suppose. I got to the lesson a tad late after lunch and was just setting up the DVD player – the previous teacher had left it on the wrong setting, so it was taking me a minute or two to work out how to fix it – when I noticed a stranger sitting at the back of the room. A man in his late fifties, wearing a crumpled, baggy grey suit. Bald on top, grey hair clipped short round the back and sides, and a pair of rimless glasses which made him look like one of those Gestapo officers you sometimes see in TV programmes.

"And what do you want?" I demanded.

"Just proceed with the lesson," he instructed. The cheek – telling me what to do in my own classroom! How dare he?

"If you're one of George Roland's minions," I calmly said to him, "Then you're in the wrong place, my friend. George informed me personally that inspection visits would finish at lunchtime today, and that my department would be exempt. *Parlez-vous français, monsieur?*"

"Film Studies," he muttered. "You were about to show a film."

"Ici, c'est la salle de français," I imperiously declared. "The Film and Media department is further down the corridor on the right."

Drawing myself up to my full height, I held my nerve, making it plain that I wasn't going to do any more until he'd left. Which he duly did.

"Not everyone can speak French as expertly as I do," I said to the class after I'd closed the door behind him. I'd planned to use that line on Thursday with my sixth form, who were expecting the results of a test, and no doubt I still would.

For the remainder of the week, the whole staff, including the head and his deputy, awaited the inspectors' report with trepidation. I, on the other hand, radiated serenity. If the others weren't optimistic, then I certainly was.

Bryant sent for me the following week. He sent for the subject heads one by one, and when my turn came, he explained that he'd read the inspectors' 'provisional report,' as he called it.

"Your department didn't get a single visit," he told me, which of course I already knew. "I don't understand why not."

"I suppose it's because my elevated reputation goes before me," I replied. "He did praise my outstanding leadership, though."

Bryant looked surprised, assuming no doubt that he alone had any idea of what Roly Poly had written. "I just can't comprehend," he spluttered, "why the inspectors are so harsh on everybody else, and yet this comment about French comes completely out of the blue.”

“Well, their word is the law,” I pointed out, as I'd heard Roly Poly himself say of cases where a head disagrees with an Ofsted judgement. “Actually, I'm in total support of Inspector Roland. A man after my own heart. Fact is, he and I have a lot in common.”

MY KING AND COUNTRY

One of the most boring parts of my job is School Assembly. I don't go to all of them, as I've usually got something far more important to do, like preparing my first lesson of the day. On some mornings I also like to go into the school office and spread a little joy among the ladies who sit there. I know how much they value my visits and the witty comments I'm kind enough to share with them.

But I have to go to some assemblies, and when I do, I always notice Marjorie, our Deputy Head, looking round and noting down on her clipboard which members of staff are in attendance. We never hear from her afterwards, but she's always there.

One morning's School Assembly was particularly tedious. Usually, Mr Bryant drones on in his long winded way, then lets one of the children do a reading or make an announcement. This time he turned the whole thing over to a girl in Year 10, Louise Caldwell. Her name will mean nothing, of course, although her older brother Tony was in the first A-Level class I taught when I was appointed to the school. Now in his final year at university, he also shows some promise as a footballer, so I'm told.

Louise told everyone that she had recently lost her great grandfather. Well into his nineties, he had been a 'D Day Veteran,' whatever that meant. From what she was saying, I think it meant he'd been a soldier in the Second World War, towards the end, probably when things were calming down a bit. A few black and white photographs, projected on the screen behind her, showed beaches with spikes and barbed wire, and other typical wartime images. I'm not interested in that kind of thing and my mind drifted to what Mrs Lee, my housekeeper, might have prepared me for my dinner that evening.

When we were eventually liberated, I could hardly believe my colleagues had attended the same assembly as I had. "Wonderful," they were saying, "How brave those young men must have been." "So vital that youngsters recognise what the wartime generation went through." "The sacrifice ..... the suffering ...... good on her for speaking out." And so it went on.

If that was the popular mood, then surely I should be at the forefront of it.

I therefore decided that I would organise an event to raise money for former soldiers, or 'veterans' as they like to be known. I know that Prince Harry has made himself extremely popular by doing exactly that, but for retired soldiers of his own generation, which is around the same age as myself, as I like to tell people. And so, I decided to be the champion of Louise's great grandfather's generation, since there was obviously considerable feeling towards that group.

I set my first class of the day a test, and while they were completing it, I considered how a fund-raiser might work. A meal, I thought, perhaps at the

Imperial Hotel where I'd recently met my old friend George Roland, who is now a Schools Inspector. An auction – people could donate their unwanted items which we could sell at no cost to ourselves – and then to top the bill, a speech by me. I'd probably call it 'My Glittering Career, by Peter Trumper' – that would surely attract the crowds more than dreary old stuff about the war. I'd have the Gazette there, I'd give an interview, and there'd be an article with, naturally, a photograph of myself. I'd be the hero of the hour!

By lunchtime, I'd got everything planned. Since I hadn't been in the school office that morning, I breezed in there as soon as the lunchtime bell rang with my list of instructions for the ladies.

"Dinner for how many at the Imperial?" they asked. "When are you having it? Where will we get the items for the auction? How will we advertise?"

Assertively, I answered all their questions. The date would be the sixth of June, which, according to my in-depth research on the internet that morning, was the anniversary of D Day itself. Quite convenient – enough time for them to get everything ready, and before the summer holidays when people might be going away. Numbers would be determined by the capacity of the hotel dining room (which the ladies could find out by making a simple phone call). To get hold of items for auction, they could phone round local shops and businesses. Advertising could be through the Gazette, local radio too, and of course the school newsletter. Nothing that would tax them beyond their capacity. I, meanwhile, would start writing my keynote address, 'My Glittering Career, by Peter Trumper.'

It didn't take much more intervention by myself, as once they had their orders, my ladies set about their task. The sixth of June was still three weeks away, but a week after giving them my instructions, I had an email from them. Here it is just as they sent it:

> Grate news! Room at Imperiel if we guarantee 50 guests – maxinum 150. Working on good hall for action. Do you want a fly-past by a Spotfire? Call Wing Commander Thorp from Royle Air Farce (RAF). Reporter from Gazzette due tomorrow – pls conform time. Kind rgrds Mo & Liz

When I send an email, I'm very careful with my spelling and punctuation, and naturally I spotted at once that either Mo or Liz had been much less so. I reminded myself to make them show me any letters they were intending to send by post. I don't think they're wholly illiterate, I am aware that a lot of emails are written in a hurry, and I knew they'd done a lot of their work by phone, so I wasn't going to call them out on their low standards in this instance.

At the end of the email there were phone numbers for the Royal Air Force man and the

Gazette, but I really felt that was something for the office ladies to be doing by themselves, so I emailed back:

> Tell Gazette to ring me at lunchtime today. Also to bring photographer. RAF can call me between 3:30 – 4:00 pm. Peter

I'll say this for the Royal Air Force: they are punctual. At 3:30 on the dot, the staffroom phone rang.

"This will be for me," I announced to those teachers who happened to be there, and I picked up the phone.

"Wing Commander Thorp for you," the lady from the office told me.

"Yes, I'll speak to him. Do put him through." I think it's good to conduct a certain number of phone calls from the staffroom – it lets my colleagues see that I'm in demand, and that contacts from the outside world are keen to seek my attention.

"Am I speaking to a Mr Trumper?" a formal voice asked.

"Yes, Peter Trumper here, Head of Modern Languages. *Enchanté, monsieur.* How may I help you?"

"Thorp, Battle of Britain Memorial Flight. I understand you'd like to book a flypast."

"Yes," I replied, "I'm told you can send me a Spotfire."

"A what?" he spluttered.

"A Spotfire. It's a kind of aeroplane, I believe." I was surprised to have to explain something so basic to him.

"You mean a Spitfire?" he asked.

"My secretary definitely said a Spotfire," I told him.

"I'm afraid we haven't got one," he said, rather drily. "We do have several Spitfires, though. That's also a type of aeroplane. Quite a famous one, so they tell me," he added.

"Well, that'll have to do, then. If one of those could trundle across just as we're about to go in for dinner –"

"Sir," he interrupted me, "Let me point out that a Spitfire does not 'trundle,' as you put it. It is, quite simply, once of the most magnificent and graceful flying machines ever built."

Somehow, I didn't feel the man was being as helpful as he could. My colleagues in the staffroom had at first been feigning indifference, but now they seemed to be paying more attention, and those that were about to leave put their bags down and looked set to stay.

"Can I just check one thing," I asked him, "You're the Wing Commander, is that right?"

"I'm Wing Commander of the Memorial Flight, yes."

"I'd want the whole aeroplane, not just the wings," I insisted. "Could I speak to the person in charge of that?"

Before answering, he made a strange gurgling noise, but when he recovered the power of speech he assured me that all flypasts are performed by a full aircraft, not just the wings, and asked me what date I wanted to book it. When I told him, he spluttered again.

"What?" he howled, "In three weeks' time? Our flying programme is set up years in advance. And do you know what day June the sixth is?"

"A Tuesday this year, I believe," I answered.

"It's the anniversary of D Day. One of the days when every aircraft we have is performing at airshows up and down this country and abroad. You could talk to me about a date next year, but not in June or September."

Despite his reluctance to assist me, I remained diplomatic and said perhaps we'd talk again later. My colleagues now started to leave, some of them shaking their heads, no doubt at Thorp's apparent inability to cooperate, and some covering their mouths as though they were about to cough.

The reporter from the Gazette phoned almost immediately afterwards, and I arranged to meet him the following day. His assistant took my photograph, and he suggested that I should write him a piece about the planned event and email it to him. It might then be edited, but at least the details would be as I wanted them to appear. I was pleased to see the following article in the next edition:

Peter Trumper masterminds D Day charity event.

Mr Peter Trumper, 32 (pictured), has organised a charity dinner on D Day, Tuesday 6th June. When interviewed, Mr Trumper, Head of Languages at the town's top secondary school, told our reporter, "Many people don't realise how much blood, sweat, toil and tears I've had to put into planning this event, but I'm sure the poor unfortunates will be deeply grateful to me."

The dinner will be held at the Imperial Hotel, starting at 7:00 pm. Tickets, priced £75 per person, are available from Mr Trumper's secretaries. There will also be an auction of splendid items, and the highlight of the evening will be a speech by Mr Trumper himself entitled 'My Glittering Career.'

The picture of me was sufficiently flattering, I thought. I may have mentioned elsewhere that I look rather like a younger version of Hugh Grant, the celebrated actor, and the resemblance was quite apparent in the photograph which had been selected.

I knew that my most important task now was the preparation of my speech. The mere mention of it in the newspaper would already be whetting my admirers' appetites. The audience would naturally want to hear again some of my more familiar anecdotes – my 'greatest hits,' if you like – but I thought some new material should also feature. Something from my student days, with the implication that I studied at Oxbridge. Maybe preparing for the Boat Race by practising my rowing skills on the River Ox. My work before I became a teacher: the time I spent as sales manager for my father's company, Trumper's IT Solutions. I knew my father wouldn't be able to attend the charity dinner, so I could be quite effusive about my achievements: salesman of the month for every month I was there, perhaps. Then I'd explain how I wanted to leave the world of Information Technology and enter the teaching profession because I didn't want people to say my resounding success was due simply to being the managing director's son.

I'd already got some good stories about the early triumphs in my teaching career. I'd used them in my interview with Mr Bryant when I applied for my position at the school, but my audience for the evening might not be so familiar with them. I most certainly needed to point out to my listeners that I am an accomplished French speaker – many would know it already, but some might not, and even for the *aficionados*, a reminder is always apt. I often tell people that whenever I visit France, everybody compliments me on my spoken French – so much so, that they think I really must be a native Frenchman! An anecdote in which that happened would certainly go down well – but who should be the one paying me the compliment? A shopkeeper? A hotelier? Maybe a local mayor? I needed to work on that story.

Some humour would also be called for. I'm well known for my witty and amusing remarks, and I wouldn't want to disappoint on this occasion. Perhaps a few choice epithets about my colleagues, Mr Simpson and Miss Jones, whose derisory attempts to speak French in no way match my own talents. Some of the stupid things parents ask me at parents' evenings, and my hilarious rejoinders. The mother who asked me how long her daughter should be spending on her French homework, to which I retorted, "Until she's finished it, of course!" Or perhaps the parents who asked me what their child needed to do to get grade A, to which I said, "A great deal more than she's doing now, *ha, ha, ha*!"

To bring things up to date, I could talk about the visit to France that I'd organised the previous year – fortunately Miss White and Miss Flowers, the two colleagues who accompanied me, had now moved on to other jobs, so they wouldn't be there to contradict my version of the story. And I could definitely tell the tale of how I'd been singled out for praise by Chief Ofsted Inspector George Roland, when everybody else's department took rather a pasting. Yes, I'd enjoy repeating that one, and even Mr Bryant would have to admit that it was the truth.

The evening of the 6th of June arrived, and just short of 150 of us gathered at the Imperial Hotel – many of them the parents of pupils at school, but the Lady Mayoress was also there, and Mr Bryant had brought a couple of the school governors. My preparations had worked out perfectly. Since I was to be giving my speech after the dinner as the star turn of the evening, I allowed Mr Caldwell – the father of Louise, the girl who had spoken in assembly – to be the host, and he was also to be the auctioneer. In the light of what was to occur later in the evening, I now realise I should have retained those roles for myself.

I have to say that at first, everything went very smoothly. Mo and Liz from the office had spent the time between the end of school and the guests' arrival helping Mr Caldwell to set up entertainments in the hotel lounge. As people enjoyed their drinks before the meal began, there was a tombola, quick-fire snooker, carpet bowls and various other contests – all with an entry fee, of course, and with small prizes to be won. When I arrived (it's never good to be too early, always best to make a dramatic entrance when the crowd is already there to see it), many guests were eagerly tackling these minor challenges, and I was pleased to see a good amount of money building up in the collection trays. Mr Bryant was an enthusiastic participant, but he took great care not to win anything, and I think beating the headmaster became a motivation for several of the more earnest competitors.

The dinner was excellent, and the service friendly and efficient. Mr Caldwell had decided to offer items for auction between the courses of the meal. To my surprise, many of the items came not in the form of goods, but as activities which had generously been donated. The ladies in the office had kept that back from me! A pleasure flight for a whole family with a pilot at the local flying club — though sadly not in a Spotfire; a round of golf with a professional player, a coaching session at the tennis club, a private box for a cup match at the football stadium, tickets for the bowling alley, the cinema, a nearby theme park and various other venues all went under the hammer. My guests got into the competitive spirit, led on by Mr Caldwell's sales patter, and I suspect many of the items went for rather more than it might have cost to buy them through the normal channels.

I congratulated myself on the amount of money I must have raised. The ladies in the office had added £25 per head to what the hotel was charging us for the meals — that's well over £3,000 — and the auction must have raised hundreds of pounds too. Surely my labours would be rewarded — how quickly should I expect to be anointed Peter Trumper, OBE? When could I expect my invitation to the Palace?

Finally, coffee was served, and I waited for my speech to be announced. I'd noticed Mr Bryant going round the tables and having a word with each set of guests, and then he approached me and said, "Just a couple more minutes." Straight after that I saw him and the two school governors disappear into the kitchens.

Seconds later they rushed out in something of a fluster, followed at similar pace by the chef and the head waiter.

"Fire! Fire!" they were shouting. "Evacuate the dining room!"

We did exactly that; outside, a fleet of taxis had already drawn up in front of the hotel, and some guests headed for them, whilst others who had come by car returned to their vehicles. The hotel staff directed those who wanted to stay towards the bar, and many followed their invitation. Nevertheless, it was clear that the main part of evening was at an end. When I realised to my *chagrin* that the gathering had broken up for good and would not reconvene, I reluctantly returned to my car and set off for home. To my further annoyance, I'd left the top down – I was still driving my BMW convertible at the time – and a shower of rain during the evening had drenched the interior, including the driver's seat. I bet the soldiers who landed on the Normandy beaches on D Day didn't have to contend with conditions like those!

Mr Bryant spoke to me at break the following morning in the staffroom. He said the evening had been a complete success, adding that the hotel had donated a further £500 to our appeal. We'd been the most decorous of guests and had cleared the premises very promptly at the finale. More awkward parties, they said, create untold damage, linger for hours and then the hotel has to pay overtime to the staff who stay behind to clear up. Bar takings for the evening had been excellent too.

To my dismay, he didn't thank me personally for all I'd done. Instead, he said he knew that Mo and Liz in the office had done all the 'spadework,' as he put it, and he thought I should have offered them complimentary tickets. If he'd known I hadn't, he said, then he'd have paid for them himself. I bridled at the suggestion. At seventy-five pounds a head, and taking place at the Imperial, the event was obviously aimed at senior managers and other professional people – certainly not secretaries and mere office staff!

The weekend edition of the Gazette came out on Friday, as it always does, and it contained the following article:

> **Hotel fire turns out to be a false alarm**
>
> A dinner on Tuesday evening at the Imperial Hotel ended slightly ahead of schedule because of a suspected fire in the hotel kitchens. The dinner was in aid of

Armed Forces charities to coincide with the anniversary of D Day.

More than one hundred and forty guests attended, and the event raised well over £8,000. Fortunately, when the fire was suspected, the evening was almost over. One of the guests, Mr Alan Caldwell, whose grandfather was a D Day veteran, said, "The evening was a complete success. We did well to avoid the closing speech, which might have delayed us for some time and put a dampener on the whole proceedings."

Headmaster Sebastian Bryant, who oversaw the event, said, "There was no conflagration, and the safety of the guests was never in jeopardy. The event had reached its natural conclusion. Many chose to continue their homage to the D Day veterans with a postprandial libation in the hotel bar, and I was honoured to be among them. A worthy tribute to an inspirational set of men and women."

Several of the guests as well as outsiders have pledged further donations because they were spared the final speeches. Proceeds from the evening could well reach a five-figure sum.

No mention of my name in all of that! How dare they? And as for the suggestion that Bryant had anything to do with organising it rather than me, well, that just shows how despicable the press really is!

I truly believe that people should honour and respect the heroes of D Day, especially the unsung ones. And there's no greater unsung hero than me, fundraiser and organiser of the evening at the Imperial Hotel, which according to the Gazette may raise as much as £10,000 for these retired old soldiers. Since most of them are dead by now, I don't know what they're planning to do with all the money, but my gallant action for King and Country should surely go down as an example to us all.

"Arise, Sir Peter?" I truly deserve it!

My Mastermind Triumph

You might not believe that for all my qualities and strengths, I still have moments of doubt.

For example, I'm far and away the most intelligent among my colleagues at school. But would they all recognise me as such, or would some of them think it was Doctor Crick, who has a PhD? Or Carol Jones, who went to Cambridge, although you wouldn't know it? I let it be known that my degree comes from the University of Oxford, and whilst everyone believes me for now, there's always the chance that someone may discover the truth and pass it on to others who really have no business to question my credentials.

My title, Mr Peter Trumper, Head of Department, implies status, and I do have people under me. But even in education, there are more prestigious posts than mine – headteachers, inspectors, chief education officers and so on. Sadly, those appointments depend on 'who you know, not what you know,' and my talent is too often overlooked.

So far as I know, I'm the only one who employs a cleaner. Her name is Mrs Lee, and she also does other menial tasks for me – cooking, laundry, ironing and so on. I still shop for myself, mind you – please don't think I have it easy! Colleagues who think they're being funny sometimes ask me why I don't marry Mrs Lee, which I find very insulting.

Admittedly, she's a widow, therefore unattached, but she's working class. She's also older than me. You'd never call her a puma, or a leopard, or whatever the word is for an attractive but mature lady. I refer to her as my housekeeper, my charlady or even my serving maid, but she is definitely not my mistress.

To show that I have something special, something which my colleagues don't, I decided to become a contestant on *Mastermind*, one of the top quiz shows on British television. I've watched it occasionally, and it doesn't look too difficult. The contestants are always boring know-all types who choose dreary subjects like science, history and books. I could not only win the trophy, but also let my exuberant wit shine through and make a mark in the world of television.

The first part – becoming a 'contender,' as they like to call it – is quite easy. I told Mo what I wanted – she's one of the women in the school office – and she entered my details on the website. It didn't worry me if she gossiped, as secretaries invariably do. If word spread at school that I was to appear on *Mastermind*, that could only enhance my reputation.

The following week, I got a call from the BBC. A lady who said she was a 'researcher' tested me with a few general knowledge questions. "You know a lot," she told me, and said I'd be hearing from them again soon.

The very next day, I had an email. "Congratulations on being shortlisted for the next series of *Mastermind!*" it ran. A producer rang me up that evening to check that I'd received the email and ask whether I'd accept. I didn't hesitate, and he asked me to name my specialist subject for my first appearance. If I got further, I'd have to choose another, but right now one would be enough.

I had, of course, thought about this beforehand. The obvious choice would be the French language, on which I must be one of the world's leading experts, but that might not produce the most interesting questions for the audience. "What is the French for potato?" I could be asked. "*Pomme de terre,*" I'd say. "Which part of the house is known in French as *la salle à manger*?" "The dining room," I'd answer. No, my chosen topic would be the *Carry On* films which I enjoy so much and would showcase my scholarly credentials. Not only do I know them intimately, having watched most of them many times over, but I could entertain the audience too. If asked, for example, for Kenneth Williams's catchphrase from *Carry On Doctor*, I could answer "Ooh, Matron!" in that whining, nasal voice that he uses. I also do an excellent version of Sid James's chortling laugh, and I can sound just like Frankie Howerd when I say, "I'm flabbergasted. My gast has never been so flabbered." If asked what Barbara Windsor was doing when she loses her bikini top, I could stand up and act out the PE exercise which causes it. As well as gaining me full marks, that would have them laughing in the studio and in their living rooms at home!

Naturally, word spread round school. "Mister Trumper's going to be on *Mastermind*," people were saying. Some even jumped the gun, assumed I'd already been on, and asked when my episode would be broadcast. "Had I won?" they asked me. I was pleased that nobody suggested a colleague who they thought might be better – not 'Luvvie' Laithwaite, the drama teacher, who might be OK on Shakespeare, but not much else; nor Headmaster Bryant, who's seen by some as a wise owl, although I don't share that opinion of the pompous old windbag; not even John Crick, who isn't really a doctor, since his PhD is in Maths, not Medicine.

A few weeks passed between my acceptance and being called to the studios. Manchester, where the programme is made, isn't a million miles from where I live and work, but I was told to report to a Manchester hotel for the Friday evening before filming. At dinner in the hotel, I sat on my own, and I think I spotted some other contestants, also solitary diners. A woman sitting at a table behind me was certainly a candidate – she must have been filmed during the day, as she got out her phone and started talking about her experience, probably to someone at home. She referred to the atmosphere in the studio and even some of the questions she'd been asked. She wasn't allowed to say how she'd performed – that was to remain secret until the episode was broadcast. I think she must have won her heat – she sounded perky and confident. Perhaps I'd encounter her in the final.

I slept well that night. Some people thought I might be nervous, but I wasn't. After breakfast on the Saturday morning, a BBC lady rounded up the four of us who were to appear together and walked us from the hotel to the studio. It's not far – studios and hotels are on the same site, and the hotels must see many guests who are due to appear on the various shows. I noticed her eyeing us up and down, presumably to check that we were suitably dressed. They don't want anything too scruffy, I'd imagine, or t-shirts with slogans, or something too revealing from the women. If my competitors dined in the same hotel as I did last night, then I must have missed them. We made general chat – I told them where I came from, all about my job, my parents and my educational background.

I suppose it's only natural to weigh up the opposition and assess one's chances. I had nothing to fear, I sensed. One young man – a university student in jeans and a plain white t-shirt – was obviously nervous and I couldn't imagine him remembering much once the questioning started. There was also a large woman in a floral dress which reminded me of a sack. She said she was unemployed, which meant she wouldn't be strong on a specialist subject, and her general knowledge would probably come from watching daytime TV. The fourth contender was an older man, bald headed and dull in his crimplene pants and brown V-neck sweater. A retired accountant, he reminded me of Captain Mainwaring from *Dad's Army*: a small personality, but with a bloated sense of self-importance.

In the studio building, we were taken to make-up, which was something I hadn't expected. My only other TV appearance was for a vox-pop interview on the seafront in Dover, when I was on my way to France with a group of pupils. People look different under studio lights, the make-up girl explained, all washed-out and bleary, so they apply some colour and eyeliner. I looked garish in the mirror, but she assured me I'd look quite natural on screen. Then out to the studio, where we were guided to our places in the line-up of four chairs. The audience was already seated, and there was polite applause for us. There was even more applause when the question master appeared, John Humphrys. That's perhaps something I should introduce at school: applause for the teacher as he enters the classroom and takes his place in front of the class. Mr Humphrys made a brief speech, welcoming us and hoping we would enjoy the experience. He then explained to the audience what would be required of them – basically shut up and sit still, but he said it in a kindly way. He does have a nice manner with the plebs, I'll give him that.

When you watch *Mastermind* on TV, you get the impression the stage is empty but for the four contestants and the presenter. Not so! Cameras, lights, all manner of people to direct you around and give instructions – it's a wonder none of this appears on screen for the viewers at home. We were told to look straight towards the camera as the introductory music played. Then to business. At some point Mr Humphrys must have explained the format of the contest – two rounds, our specialist subject followed by general knowledge – and that in the event of a tie, the number of 'passes', or non-attempts to answer a question, would be taken into consideration. I don't remember him saying it, but I was probably thinking ahead to my performance in the contestants' chair.

I was the first contender, since I was seated on the far right, or the left as it would appear on TV. If I'd realised this beforehand, I'd have told them to change it. It would surely make for a huge anticlimax as I charged ahead to a great score which no one else could even approach, as well as entertaining the audience with my quickfire repartee and *Carry On* impersonations. Shouldn't I go last, the 'top of the bill,' surging ahead of my vanquished rivals one by one as my score overtook theirs?

But there was no opportunity to put this right. Instead, I walked assuredly down the gangway to the contestants' chair. Facing me, Mr Humphrys asked me my name, profession and specialist subject. "Peter Trumper, Head of Department. The *Carry On* films," I confidently replied. Mr Humphrys repeated, presumably for the audience's benefit, "The *Carry On* films, a series of 31 British comedies mainly from the 1960s and 70s. Peter

Trumper, you have two minutes on the *Carry On* films."

Later, the BBC sent me a private link to my segment from the show. They insisted no-one else should see it before the programme was transmitted, as they like to maintain the illusion of a live broadcast. I've re-watched it several times, so I can guarantee that my account is accurate, and I can remember exactly what I was thinking as I responded to each question.

JOHN HUMPHRYS: "Which was the earliest *Carry On* film, released in 1958?"

I'd never thought of the films in any particular order, I'd just thought of them as being from the 1960s and 70s, as Mr Humphrys had said in his introduction. As for the earliest ...... I've never heard of one called *Carry On Caveman*, so I confidently declared, "*Carry On Cleopatra.*"

JH: "No, it was *Carry On Sergeant*. Which *Carry On* scriptwriter made his debut with *Carry On Cabbie* and went on to write a further 19 films in the series? He also wrote *Up Pompeii* for the actor Frankie Howerd."

I'd always assumed there was a team of writers, rather than just one. I couldn't name any of them, so I passed, even though I know it's best to guess if you can.

JH: "In which 1960 film did Sid James, who went on to star in 18 further *Carry On* films, make his series debut?"

There was my first chance to entertain the audience. Sid James was in a lot of *Carry On* films, so I guessed "*Carry On Cabbie,*" and added a hearty "*Arf, arf, arf!*" for good measure. The audience failed to respond. Mr Humphrys looked a bit concerned, but quickly continued.

JH: "It was *Carry On Constable*. Until *Carry On Emmanuelle*, rated AA and therefore banned to children under the age of 14, what British Board of Film Classification rating was applied to every other film in the series?"

Now that was an obvious one. Straight away, I said "U – Universal Access," and then I added, "A bit like my housekeeper, *ha, ha, ha!*" Mr Humphrys flinched; I think they must have muffled the sound of the audience's laughter, and he kept going.

JH: "No, it was 'A – children only if accompanied by an adult.' Which 1964 film was to have been named *Carry On Up The Armada*, before the British Board of Film Censors rejected the title?"

I know there was a film based around the Spanish Armada, but I couldn't think of its title. Remembering the advice not to say 'Pass' if possible, I tried: "*Carry On Sailor.*"

JH: "That's close – it was *Carry On Jack*. Who wrote the music for 23 of the 31 *Carry On* films?"

Now that was a mean question! Who watches the *Carry On* films for the music? Again, I had to say, "Pass."

JH: "In *Carry On Cleo*, Julius Caesar, played by Kenneth Williams, has a famous line: 'Infamy, infamy, they've all got it in for me.' Who was he speaking to at the time?"

Now that's a celebrated moment! But Mr Humphrys sounded nothing like Kenneth Williams, so I drew an intake of breath through my nostrils and, in my best impersonation, which I know is uncannily accurate, I whined, "Infamy, infamy, they've all got it in for me!" Once again, they must have filtered out the audience's laughter. My Humphrys glanced towards the producer and asked me:

JH: "Who was Julius Caesar speaking to?"

An unfair question, I thought. All eyes are surely on Kenneth Williams at that point – after all, he's the star! So, I guessed. "Was it Cleopatra?"

JH: "No, it was the bodyguard Bilius. Mr Trumper, please try and answer the question if you can," he added, before resuming with: "Which 1961 film, number 5 in the series, was the first not to have the title *Carry On* followed by a job or profession?"

That's hard! Most of them have jobs in the title: *Carry On Doctor, Nurse, Cowboy, Matron* .... and many more. I knew time must be running out.

If I said "Pass," perhaps there would be time for one more question. So, I did.

JH: "In *Carry On Spying*, what is the name of the secret agent played by Charles Hawtrey?" Suddenly, the buzzer sounded, enabling Mr Humphrys to use his famous catchphrase, "I've started, so I'll finish." He continued, "The character's name had to be changed from James Bind because the producers of the James Bond franchise threatened legal action."

That buzzer was a bit of a gift – I knew I could take my time over my answer. I rolled the phrase around, sounding every inch the Sean Connery as I said, "The name'sh Bond, Jamesh Bond." Once again, the audience's sounds of appreciation and applause must have been edited out. But if it wasn't James Bind, what else could it be? James Band? James Bend? I just couldn't remember. Finally, when Mr Humphrys prompted me with, "I must have an answer," I chose "James Blonde," even though I know Charles Hawtrey certainly wasn't blonde.

JH: "It was Charlie Bind. You passed on three. The scriptwriter who also wrote for Frankie Howerd was Talbot Rothwell, the composer was Eric Rogers, and the first *Carry On* film without a profession in the title was *Carry On Regardless*. At the end of that round, Peter Trumper, you have no points. But not to worry, you'll have your chance again with the general knowledge."

I trudged back to my chair, directed by an assistant who must have known exactly where to stand to remain unseen by the cameras. My chances of winning were seriously reduced, although perhaps the other contestants would also score badly on their specialist subjects, and I knew I'd be strong in the second round, since my general knowledge is superb.

I didn't pay close attention to the other three contestants, and there isn't a digital scoreboard like there is on TV. But I knew they were all answering at least some of their questions correctly. A couple of times an assistant had to call for filming to stop when I found my chair uncomfortable and needed to wriggle or stretch out. That happened once as the large woman was returning to her chair, so she had to return to the spotlight and repeat her walk back to contestants' row. The exercise would do her good, I commented, but sadly the microphone wasn't on me at the time.

John Humphrys announced round two. As in round one, I was the first to be called. Ten was now the score to beat, he said, and then the questions began again.

JOHN HUMPHRYS: "Mick Fleetwood and John McVie were both founder members of which long-running British pop group?"

A bad one to start! I don't know many pop groups. I know it wasn't The Beetroots or The Stoned Rollers, as I wittily like to call them, so I quickly said "Pass," hoping the next question would be easier.

JH: "What do all competitors in the Invictus Games have in common?"

I knew that! "Well, they're not board games or card games, they're definitely sports. So, they're all sportsmen," I affirmed. "And women," I added. Mr Humphrys said I needed to be more specific, so I said, "Athletics." He didn't make any comment; he just moved on to the next question.

JH: "What nickname was given to 617 Squadron of the Royal Air Force following its first successful bombing mission over Nazi Germany in May 1943?"

Easy! I saw them on television recently, flying over Buckingham Palace. "The Red Arrows!" I immediately called out.

JH: "No, it was the Dam Busters. What name is given to the assembly of cardinals in the Roman Catholic Church who meet to elect a new pope?"

I don't follow church events. I know the story about the white smoke from the chimney, but I don't know who sets it off. "The Parish Council," I guessed.

JH: "The Conclave. Which Roman Emperor was said to have fiddled while Rome burned?"

I thought about how all the Romans had funny names. Bilius was Kenneth Williams's bodyguard in *Carry On Cleo*. Frankie Howerd played the servant

Lurcio, who used to lurk about. His master was Ludicrus, who was married to Ammonia. There was a Nausius too.

"He fiddled," I pondered, working out what the answer might be. "It must have been …….. Violinius."

JH: "It was Nero. An older, sexually attractive woman is often referred to as which member of the cat family?"

I was thinking about this recently when someone had asked me about Mrs Lee, and I knew puma and leopard were both wrong. "A lioness?" I suggested.

JH: "No, that's an England women's footballer."

"A footballer isn't a cat," I complained. "You asked me to name a type of *cat*!"

JH: "Pause the clock, please. The species of cat is a cougar. The nickname 'lionesses' is given to the England women's football team. Next question: The Impressionist art movement took its name from the 1872 painting *Impression Sunrise* by which French artist?"

John Humphrys has his qualities, but he clearly isn't a French speaker. "That's *Impression Soleil*," I corrected him, in what I knew was my perfect French. Instead of thanking me, he simply repeated the question: "Who painted *Impression Soleil Levant*?"

"I know so many French artists," I explained, "I'm quite an expert. There's Toulouse Lautrec, Picasso – no, he's Spanish – I'm sure there's one called Croissant, or it might be Vol-au-Vent." At that moment the buzzer sounded again, and Mr Humphrys insisted, "And you must now answer." I did; I went for Van Gogh.

JH: "It was Claude Monet. You passed on two: the British pop group founded by Mick Fleetwood and John McVie was Fleetwood Mac, and competitors at the Invictus Games are disabled ex-servicemen. Peter Trumper, at the end of round two, and this was bound to happen one day – we've been doing Mastermind since 1972 – you still have no points. And the next contender, please."

I was going to walk straight to the lounge, but the assistant once again directed me back to my chair in contestants' row. I had to sit there as the other three contenders went forward to answer their questions. They all got several right, a few wrong, and passed once or twice, but from a starting position which was already in front of mine, they were bound to finish ahead of me. John Humphrys announced the winner – it was the student, who was less nervous on stage than he had been prior to filming – and then the audience clapped, and we were all ushered back to the waiting area.

A floor manager tapped me on the arm and asked me to come back on set. By now, the house lights had been switched on and the spotlights dimmed.

The audience had left, apart from a few stragglers who were still shuffling out through the studio doors. John Humphrys remained seated behind his presenter's desk, where he'd been joined by the show's producer.

The producer wanted to know whether I was happy for the episode to be aired. Would being the first ever contender to score zero be upsetting to me? Unprepared, I nonetheless came up with a very good suggestion. I generously said I'd be prepared to film my two rounds again. Whilst I couldn't remember all the answers I'd been given when mine were wrong or when I'd passed, I could certainly remember enough to produce a creditable score, maybe even a winning one. And delight the viewers again with my quickfire wit and hilarious *Carry On* impersonations.

That wasn't what the producer had in mind, although it was obviously the best solution. They didn't want to let me have another go, and if I preferred to duck out, then a substitute would have to be found. One was available: it was Erica, one of the usherettes, who would be given the same questions as me, but with strict instructions not to answer more than the three other candidates who now knew their finishing positions. They were marched back into the studio and seated on contestants' row with Erica taking my place on the left. She was then filmed twice walking past them to the contestants' chair and back again, each time with a nervous smile about her face. At that point we were all dismissed. The sequences with Erica answering the questions would be filmed in private before the audience was admitted for the next round, and the whole thing would be edited to make it look as if she'd been the original participant throughout.

When the series started on TV, people asked me when my episode would be shown. Word had spread, and I may even have mentioned it myself before the filming took place. Sure enough, the episode was screened, with Erica as an engaging but uninspired first contestant. As instructed, she took fourth place, coming in five points behind the winner. It was perfectly edited; you'd never have guessed that she was a last-minute addition.

I may not have scored many points, but I came up with a superb piece of imaginative fiction. On reflection, I realise that's a far more important skill than being able to rattle off a few random facts about famous pop groups, or Royal Air Force squadrons, or fusty old paintings. Where would I be without my talent for invention? Would I have my prestigious job? Would I be such a consummate speaker of so many foreign languages? Would I be held in such esteem by my pupils, my colleagues and by schools inspector George Roland?

But how could I explain that I'd never appeared on *Mastermind* despite having told everybody I was going to?

After considerable thought, I can now present the true facts. My episode was never shown for the following reasons: first, the BBC always films more programmes than it intends to broadcast, because sometimes in the studio things go wrong. Maybe the lighting isn't right, or there's too much background noise, which prevents an episode from being aired. In my case, it was the audience's laughter at my witticisms and their applause for my impersonations that drowned out some of what was being said. Second, I won my episode very comfortably, and it wasn't broadcast simply because there wasn't enough tension; the result was too obvious from the start.

Everyone I spoke to believed me. And over the course of time, I even came to believe it myself. My *Mastermind* triumph would become a legend.

Marcel Proust and I

Editor's note: Readers will appreciate, as Peter Trumper apparently failed to do, the coincidence that two people were called Stephen Hudson. One of them taught for a while in my school and is alive to this day. The other translated some of Marcel Proust's works into English, notably 'Le temps retrouvé' (the final volume of 'A la recherche du temps perdu') when the original translator, C K Scott-Moncrieff, died leaving the English version incomplete.

Unlike my former colleague, Proust's translator was not really called Stephen Hudson. That was a pen name; he was christened Sydney Schiff. He knew Proust well, particularly in Proust's latter years, corresponded with him, and was the host on a celebrated occasion in early 1922 when Proust met other luminaries such as James Joyce, Pablo Picasso and Igor Stravinsky.

Sebastian Bryant

In my distinguished career, I've managed several junior colleagues. Very few remain under my authority for very long! I've mentioned Mary White and Ann Flowers, who accompanied me on the highly successful visit I organised to France, when my timely interventions prevented what could easily have been a calamity. I currently have two subordinates: Bob Simpson and Carol Jones. I always enjoy pointing out that Mr Simpson has never been to France, in contrast to my own visits when I'm welcomed as a native and acclaimed for my outstanding command of the language. Miss Jones, who joined my department only recently, is a strange, desperate woman who locks herself away with her books on the days she isn't contracted to come into school. Very pretty, went to Cambridge, but she teaches her pupils absolutely nothing.

I haven't mentioned Stephen Hudson, who worked under me for a couple of years when other candidates were in short supply. Naturally, his French was never a patch on mine, but I resented him most for his total lack of deference. I gave him all the German classes as well as a few in French. My German is truly superb, and I'm fluent in Italian too, as I proved so memorably when I dined at *La Dolce Vita* with Ofsted Inspector George Roland. But it's a strain to have to prepare lessons in more than one language, so I made sure I kept only French classes for myself.

As their superior – professionally, socially and intellectually – I always like to know a little bit about my underlings. That's why I set out one Saturday morning to drive past Mr Hudson's house on my way to the shops. It's in a working class neighbourhood, and I could see his wife hanging out washing in the back garden. I had to get out of my car to watch her through a side gate, and I found it quite astonishing to see a woman doing her own household chores. Doesn't she have a cleaner, like I do? I know it was his wife, because once she'd hung out the washing, she sat down in a deckchair with a glass of mineral water and started to read a paperback novel!

When I got home, I looked him up on Google, as I do for most people I encounter – other teachers, parents, and so on. There's never much to find out – bland, all of them, but for Mr Hudson, it was very different. According to Wikipedia, which is a totally reliable source, he's an associate of a French writer called Marcel Proust, and has translated some of his books into English.

I was, of course, immediately familiar with Marcel Proust – no need for me to look *him* up on Google! As I often tell my classes, he wrote a famous book called *Je cherche le temps perdu* which I've read many times. A lot of people find it difficult and struggle to understand it, but for me it's quite straightforward.

But I couldn't understand how Mr Hudson came to be the translator of a well-known novel which has no doubt made its author a great deal of money. My French is far better than his – surely, I should be the one translating it for English readers!

I decided to ask Mr Hudson about this. Association with a celebrated French novelist would reflect well on me too! I caught him in the staffroom first thing on Monday morning.

"Steve," I asked him. I adopted a familiar tone, knowing that people whose first name is Stephen prefer to be known as 'Steve' by their most valued acquaintances. "Steve," I said, "how well do you know Marcel Proust?"

"Not as well as I'd like," he said. "I've read *A la recherche*, some of his correspondence too, but there's a whole lot more. What do you want to know about him?"

"Well," I enquired, "how often do you see him? I'd like you to introduce him to me next time you meet up."

Steve looked at me a bit strangely – he clearly wanted to keep his friend to himself, and realised that if I appeared on the scene, Mr Proust would surely see me as a far superior partner and a much better translator for his future writings.

"You want to meet him?" he asked, with a touch of alarm.

"Of course I do. I'm sure he'd be thrilled to meet me too," I confirmed.

"Let me think about it. I'll get back to you in few days' time," Steve promised. "You really think you'd hit it off with him?"

The following week, I reminded Mr Hudson of his promise. "If you're still keen," he told me, "Marcel said he's coming over this weekend. He likes to visit the French Bistro – you know, the café near the station. I'm meeting him there at 3 o'clock on Saturday. You could join us if you like."

I dislike the French Bistro, but I didn't say so. On my one previous visit, I found the staff surly, rude, and totally unappreciative of my outstanding French when I placed my order. I'd walked out saying I was never going back there. "*Je ne serai pas venir ici encore*," I'd told them in no uncertain terms, which means "I shan't be coming here again."

The following Saturday, the place was quite busy, and Steve had done well to find a seat at a table with two more empty chairs. He rose to greet me and poured me a coffee from the pot that was already on the table. On his signal, a waitress brought me a cream doughnut – my favourite of all the cakes.

"Isn't Marcel here yet?" I asked. If Steve is on first name terms with the Frenchman, then surely I should be too.

"Yes, he's on his way," Steve said. "Give him a few minutes."

Sure enough, a couple of minutes later, the doorbell tinkled and in walked what was clearly Mr Proust. A smallish, slightly built man with a warm smile. He certainly looked like a writer: a dapper, old-fashioned look, lacquered hair with a central parting, a waxed moustache which pointed slightly upwards at the ends. He wore a tight, narrow-cut suit, buttoned high on his chest, and a bow tie. A scholarly demeanour, and obviously someone who didn't go out much in the modern world.

Steve again stood to greet him, and I was about to pour him a coffee from the pot, but he held up his hand. Instead, he called over one of the waitresses, addressing her softly as *"Mademoiselle, s'il vous plaît."* I didn't overhear what he ordered from her, but she soon returned with a pot of tea and a plate of madeleine cakes.

Steve introduced me. *"Marcel, mon collègue, Peter Trumper."* I was annoyed to be described as a mere 'colleague' when in truth I'm his line manager and superior, but that's just another example of Steve's lack of deference. *"Peter Trumper, tête de département des langues modernes. Enchanté, monsieur,"* I greeted him.

"Please, you can speak to me in English," he said. "I am often in England, and some of my work is with English too."

He spoke good English, I thought – not as perfect as my French, naturally, but tolerable, despite a mild French accent. He continued, "Mister Trumper, my friend Stephen has told me so much about you. I feel as though I know you already."

"*Ah, toute bon, j'expecte,*" I wittily replied.

"Mister Trumper, please do not try to speak French with me today. I am tired, I have had a long journey," he said. "Last night in my hotel I did not sleep well. I missed my goodnight kiss from my mother."

I knew at once that he'd benefit from some of my sound advice. I always wake up in the best of spirits, as I explained to him in my perfect French, because I know how important it is to sleep on a high-quality mattress.

"You are a homosexual?" Marcel asked.

"*Certainement pas!*" I retorted. "How dare you suggest that!"

"It is because you said you sleep on top of a very comfortable sailor," he replied.

I most definitely said no such thing. I checked in my pocket dictionary when I got home, and the two words are quite similar, *matelot* and *matelas*. But I can't possibly have used the wrong one – I would never make a mistake like that.

"To bat for the other side is more common than we think," Marcel went on. "In these times, it is quite acceptable. Much more so than in my day."

"It's not acceptable to me," I insisted. "I'd be horrified if anyone thought I was gay. It's abhorrent."

"Of course," Marcel agreed. "Please excuse me for intruding on a private matter. Let me change the subject. When I meet someone new, I like to know what they think about the important questions in life. Tell me, what is your opinion of Dreyfus?"

He looked at me quizzically and awaited my considered reply. At the same time, he poured himself a cup of tea – no milk – before taking a madeleine from the plate. After dipping it in the warm liquid, he bit off the dampened end, rolled it around his tongue and then swallowed it. "Ah, the precious essence, the all-powerful joy. It reminds me of when I was a young boy, on that cold winter's day with my mother," he mused. He seemed to drift away into reverie. Then suddenly he came to himself and insisted, "But what of Dreyfus, Mister Trumper?"

For those who don't know, Chief Inspector Dreyfus, played by the actor Herbert Lom, was Inspector Clouseau's boss in the *Pink Panther* films, starring Peter Sellers. Faced with Clouseau's comic incompetence, he goes mad, which leads to even more comedy.

"I felt sorry for him at first," I said, "but his insanity makes him much less sympathetic."

"And why do you think Dreyfus was insane?" Proust asked me. "Is it insane for a Jew who lives in France to serve in the French army, to defend his homeland?"

If Chief Inspector Dreyfus is Jewish, that doesn't come across in the films. Nor is the audience told whether he was a military man before joining the police. I know the *Pink Panther* films very well; along with the *Carry On* series, also from the 1960s and 70s, they're my favourite choice of entertainment on DVD. Mr Proust, on the other hand, seemed to be out of his depth, but he persisted. "Are you not moved by '*J'accuse,*' Zola's condemnation of how Dreyfus was treated by the French establishment?" he wanted to know.

Of course I was aware of Gianfranco Zola, an Italian footballer who played for Chelsea a few years ago, but I said I had no idea what he thought about the *Pink Panther* movies.

Steve intervened, saving Mr Proust's embarrassment. "I think you're talking about two different people," he commented.

I wanted to show Mr Proust that I was familiar with his work, and that Steve wasn't the only one who could translate for him. "I do admire your books, Mr Proust, especially your latest one, *Je cherche le temps perdu*," I said to him.

"But you are too kind," he replied, with a modest shrug. "Do you not find it a little self-indulgent? Are its themes so vitally important?"

"Absolutely," I enthused. "When I was a child, we had blazing hot summers and cold, freezing winters with real snow at Christmas. A book looking for the lost weather of days gone by is just what we need. *Le temps perdu*, indeed. I shall certainly read it again."

Marcel had just the time to say, "*Où sont les neiges d'antan?*" before he coughed and spluttered. The dunked madeleine must have tickled his throat, but he hastily dipped it back into his black tea and took another mouthful. "Please, take one," he gasped, pointing to the remaining cakes on the plate. "But with coffee, I don't think the effect would be quite the same."

"Have you written many books?" I asked. If I was to be engaged as his translator, I felt it was important to show an interest in other work he might have produced.

"Only a few," he admitted. "Personally, I think my best work is on Ruskin. I do enjoy Ruskin."

From his pronunciation, I worked out that he was trying to make a verb out of 'a rusk', which is a type of cake, possibly a bit easier to digest than the madeleine which now seemed to be causing him some discomfort. "Me too," I agreed. "I like rusking. But here in England, you can't beat a good old fashioned cream doughnut."

Proust spluttered again, and Steve also took one of the madeleines from the plate and stuffed it into his mouth. Like Marcel, he remained speechless for a good while.

We stayed a little longer. I shared with Marcel my extensive knowledge of French culture – my many visits, my taste in French food and wine, my preference for French clothes. I dropped in names to underline my familiarity: *Paris, la Tour Eiffel, Jean-Paul Gaultier, Pierre Cardin*, and I explained the difference between a *croissant* and a *pain au chocolat*. I even tried one of his madeleine cakes – quite individual, with a nutty, marzipan taste – but I didn't dunk it in my coffee. I've never heard of French people doing that – it must be an eccentricity of Marcel's. The café was busy, with the *venir-et-aller*, as we French speakers like to call it, of

133

customers arriving and leaving in a steady flow. The two waitresses, in their blue and white stripy tops that I remembered from my first visit, were constantly rushing about, noting down and fetching fresh orders. They weren't surly, like the two young men I remembered from last time, but seemed friendly, full of smiles, and happy to be addressed in English by those customers who, unlike me, had little command of the French language.

I'd just finished explaining why, despite my love of all things French, I tend to go for German cars – BMW and Audi – rather than their French counterparts like Citroën and Renault, which are usually cheaper and less prestigious, when Marcel and Steve said they had to leave. I decided to stay – I'd have another of the doughnuts and another coffee. I told them I'd sit and read a book, which is a very French thing to do in a café, and I'd feel like an intellectual, like Jean-Luc Godot, Simon de Beaver or Jean-Paul somebody-or-other. Marcel asked me what I was currently reading, and I hoped he wasn't going to ask to see it, because all I had in my bag was a Marks & Spencer's catalogue. I said I was perusing *L'Etranger*, which means *The Foreigner*, but I wasn't enjoying it because I think French books should be about proper French people, not foreigners. Not as though I've ever read one, but I have heard the name of Albert Musak. I didn't want to say I was reading something by Mr Proust himself, because he'd probably ask me questions about it which I wouldn't be able to answer.

Shortly after Steve and Marcel left, a single gentleman came in and headed towards my table. I assumed he was going to ask if one of the two other chairs was free, but he didn't.

"Mister Peter Trumper?" he asked. "I wonder if you'd mind coming with me." He took a police officer's warrant card from his inside pocket, holding it carefully down beside the table so that other customers wouldn't see it. I hadn't picked him out as a policeman; he was neatly dressed, if rather conservatively, and his light sandy hair was tidy and well-trimmed.

I know that my junior colleague Carol Jones sometimes does translation work for the police, with illegal immigrants and such like, so I naturally assumed I was being invited to take over from her. I am, as everybody knows, a far better speaker of French than she is, and I really can't think why she got the work in the first place. If the café's other customers saw me leaving, they'd naturally think I was being called away to an important meeting. Being ushered away by an officer in uniform would have been interpreted quite differently!

The policeman led me to his car and opened the passenger door for me. Once he was in the driver's seat and we'd set off, he introduced himself as

Detective Constable Phillips. As for why I was required at the police station, he said he'd tell me when we got there.

I was taken into a small interview room where we were joined by a young and attractive looking policewoman in uniform. The two officers sat facing me across a Formica-topped table. "Where's the culprit?" I asked, expecting that my French-speaking skills were about to be called upon.

"Mr Trumper," the plainclothes man addressed me, "we've received complaints about some offensive comments you've been making which may constitute a hate crime."

"What?" I protested, "I haven't said anything. I haven't committed a crime, and I don't hate anybody. What's this all about?"

"I'm talking specifically about comments you made this afternoon in the French Bistro on Station Road," the officer replied.

"I was at the French Bistro," I said. "That's where you found me. I'd been having coffee with two acquaintances. Surely you're not saying they reported me?"

"No, sir, the complaints came from customers at adjoining tables who recognised you and overheard what you were saying," the policeman explained.

"Tell me who these people are and why they think they're entitled to listen to my private conversations," I insisted.

He refused to answer me. "Mister Trumper, the complainants have the right to remain anonymous." A feeble excuse if ever I heard one! They recognised me – my status as a local celebrity easily explains that – but surely I should be entitled to know their names too. Quite unfairly, DC Phillips begged to disagree.

He took out a notebook and flicked through it. Settling on a page with some handwritten notes, he summarised, "Your comments relate specifically to finding homosexuals 'abhorrent;' to stating your opinion that Jews are 'insane;' and finally, to proclaiming your belief that books should not be written about foreigners. That's homophobia, antisemitism and racism. I'm afraid I must warn you that –"

"You're misquoting me," I protested. "I said none of those things. If some stupid old git misheard me, then that isn't my fault!"

"Sir, please don't add ageism to the list," the policeman interrupted. "I can assure you that no-one is accusing you of a crime. It's simply that your comments were taken as offensive, and in that light I must advise you –"

"I'm not having that," I insisted. "I merely said that I'd find it abhorrent to be accused of homosexuality myself. What other consenting adults do in private is their own affair. I said that Chief Inspector Dreyfus goes mad, and anyone who watched *The Pink Panther Strikes Again* would certainly agree with me. Is he supposed to be Jewish? I don't see it that way – there's no sign of it. As for foreigners, I was criticising a book called *L'Etranger*, saying I prefer French novels to be set in France and about French people. That's a perfectly reasonable preference."

"I understand, sir," the officer acknowledged, breathing a sigh, "but not everyone sees it from your point of view. May I ask who had been with you in the café?"

"Yes, it was my junior colleague Stephen Hudson and the French author Marcel Proust," I answered. I didn't want to be uncooperative with the police, even though I was quite insulted by the detective's accusations.

"Would that be the Marcel Proust of *A la recherche du temps perdu*?" he asked. "And you say you had coffee with him this afternoon?"

"Exactly. In fact, Marcel drank tea. What's more, he dunked his madeleine cake in it, which is something I would never do," I added.

"Mister Trumper, I think we've heard all we need," Constable Phillips informed me, exchanging a glance with the WPC who seemed to be trying hard to suppress a fit of coughing. There must be a bug going about; Marcel and Steve had it too. "As I say," Phillips continued, "no crime has been committed, but in future you do need to be more guarded when making comments in public spaces which may be misinterpreted. Thank you for giving up your time. And now, WPC Andrews here will be happy to offer you a lift home."

And that was it, my first ever brush with the law. I still can't see what Detective Constable Phillips was driving at, since I was stating pure facts, as I always do. I never give offence with anything I say. I may criticise those who fail to uphold my own high standards, but I always express myself in purely objective terms. And in suggesting I was being homophobic, antisemitic or racist, the eavesdroppers were merely betraying their own ignorance and stupidity.

I'm not one to name-drop, but I do believe my acquaintance with Marcel Proust must have worked in my favour with the local constabulary. They say, "It's not what you know, it's who you know," and my being on first name terms with a famous French author must have impressed them.

Much to my annoyance, the local police still prefer to use Carol Jones when they need a French interpreter, and I don't know why that should be. Moreover, for some reason which I can't figure out, Marcel has never got back to me about translating the rest of his books into English. They just don't know what they're missing!

All the same, as I was telling Mr Bryant just the other day, sharing tea and cakes with Marcel Proust is something that not many of us can boast about!

The Joys of Fatherhood

There can be few feelings to match the joy of becoming a father for the first time. I don't just mean the conception – I'm talking about the birth too. It's a time of hope: how will my baby turn out? Will it share my good looks? Will it admire me and try to live up to my qualities and strengths? Will it one day make me proud of its achievements in the classroom and on the sports field?

Of course, it helps if you know something about the baby. Is it a boy or a girl? Where is it? Who is its mother?

My thoughts were prompted by a letter I recently received. It was one of those rare occasions when the postman knocked at my door. Normally, he simply drops his deliveries through the letter box. I went to answer.

"Mister Trumper?" he asked.

"Yes, that's me, Peter Trumper."

"I've got a letter for you, sir, but there's a delivery charge of ten pounds," he explained.

I told him sharply that the Royal Mail doesn't work that way – it's the sender who pays by purchasing stamps and sticking them onto the item being sent. But he ignored my protestations. In this case, he said, the sender had underpaid by attaching a stamp of too little value.

I continued to object. £10.00 is far more than the cost of sending a letter – even at today's ridiculous prices – and the envelope in his hand looked no larger or heavier than a standard item. Anyway, why should I pay? How did I know it was intended for me?

Postie tried to explain. The item was addressed to me: my name and address were correct. The £10.00 fee was calculated by taking the difference between the sender's stamp and the correct price, plus a service charge. But what if it was junk mail, I asked, some sort of advertising leaflet for a product I didn't want to buy? I'd be paying a tenner for something which would go straight into the dustbin. "The paper recycling bin, I'd hope, sir," he said. Frankly, that didn't help.

I asked him to open the envelope and tell me what it contained and who it was from. Then I could reasonably decide whether I wanted it or not. No, he told me, he wasn't allowed to do that. Frustrated, I asked him what would happen if I refused to pay. "The letter would go back to the sorting office," he explained. "There, it would be opened in order to identify the sender, to whom it would be returned."

"But that's a whole load of extra work," I pointed out. "Why not simply get rid of it by dumping it in my letter box?"

Complain as I might, he wouldn't budge. I thought of asking him if he could hold it up to the light to see what it might be, then snatching it, running inside and slamming the door in his face, but in the end, I handed over my £10.00, for which he gave me a receipt, and received my letter.

I had no idea what it could be, as there was nothing I was expecting. It was in a plain white envelope, on which 'Mr P Trumper' and my address were handwritten. A personal letter, then, but not from somebody who addresses me by my first name. Neat, tidy writing, the rounded letters suggesting a female hand. It bore a local postmark, but the rest of the franking was smudged, either by handling or by having been exposed to the winter damp.

Intrigued, I tore it open. Inside was a single sheet of paper, folded in two. Unfolding it revealed a short message, in the same handwriting as the envelope. There was no sender's address, and no surname.

> Dear Mister Trumper – Our little bundle of joy arrived earlier today. I know it must be from you. Settling in and doing well! We have chosen the name 'Kimba.'
>
> With all my thanks,
>
> Marian

My first thought was that I couldn't possibly be a father. I know what men do to become one, but for me the opportunity had never arisen. Could it have happened without my knowledge, though? Maybe after a few glasses too many of my favourite *Pinot Grigio*? And yet I couldn't recall a recent occasion on which I'd had more than a single glass. I remembered the time when George 'Roly Poly' Roland had drunk a lot more than me at an Italian restaurant (and I, completely sober, had driven home); I'd had a glass with some of my meals when I took my pupils on a visit to France (although I'd only made it as far as Dover); and when I organised the D Day commemoration dinner I didn't touch a drop, as I'd been preparing to deliver my after dinner speech.

Some say ignorance is possible, however. Prince Andrew, the Duke of York, claimed in an interview to have no recollection of meeting, let along sleeping with, Virginia Roberts, as she was then known, even though she clearly remembered the three occasions on which it had happened. And given her profession, I'd have thought she would be the one to forget most of her encounters after a certain length of time.

Then it occurred to me that the message could be a scam. I don't know anyone called Marian — at least, not of childbearing age. Some of my younger pupils may be called that, but the letter couldn't have come from any of them. Perhaps there was no 'Marian' and no baby either; the whole thing might be a prelude to asking me for money to see pictures of 'my' baby, or to demanding maintenance costs for a child who didn't exist or who had nothing to do with me. There was even the possibility of blackmail: 'Marian' could threaten to expose me as the father of an illegitimate child unless I paid for the information to be concealed. But there was such a sweet tone to the message that I simply couldn't accept it wasn't genuine.

I found it odd that the message referred to "our bundle of joy" – 'us' presumably being the mother and I – but then it said, "We have chosen the name." Shouldn't the father be part of that decision too? So who else apart from Marian had helped to make the choice?

Intrigued, I decided to phone the maternity ward at the local hospital. The postmark was local, so the mother must be from round these parts. The note said the baby was born 'earlier today,' so even if it had taken a couple of days in the post, there was every chance the mother was still in the post-natal ward.

"Good morning," I said to the receptionist, "I'm enquiring about the welfare of a new-born baby."

"Your name, sir?" she asked.

"Trumper, Mister Peter Trumper," I replied.

There was a pause, before the lady came back, "I'm afraid we haven't got a Mrs Trumper in the ward."

"No, of course not," I said, "the mother and I aren't married. She's called Marian."

"Do you have a surname for her?" the receptionist asked.

"No, I don't. But the baby was born either yesterday or the day before," I explained.

"I'm sorry, sir," she replied, "but we can give out information only to immediate family. Data protection rules. If you can't identify the mother, then I'm afraid I'm unable to help you any further."

I had expected something like this. I had little information to give, and even less to prove that I was a legitimate enquirer, namely the father of the child. I could go to the hospital, though, and visit the maternity ward. If 'Marian' was an acquaintance, I'd surely recognise her. I set off straight after lunch, taking with me one of my special cards to offer the new mother. My special cards feature a portrait of myself, a smaller version of the picture which hangs in my hallway, taken a few years ago by a professional photographer at his private studio, with space for a personal message on the inside. I didn't write an inscription for the time being, thinking I might add something appropriate once I knew who the mother was.

So, mid-afternoon, I arrived at the hospital. There were various car parks, each announcing an exorbitant charge. Furthermore, you had to know exactly how long you were going to spend there – one hour, two hours, or more – and pay for that length of time. Fortunately, I spotted a parking area marked 'Surgeons only'. A large Mercedes was just entering, and I was able to follow it through the barrier. I parked well away from it, though; I didn't want the driver to challenge me about my right to be there. That's one benefit of having a stylish car such as my BMW convertible: I can park where I like, and attendants will assume I'm a person of status, and therefore entitled to a parking spot.

Approaching the maternity ward, I was confused by two separate signs: ante-natal and neo-natal. 'Ante-natal' must mean contraception, since anti-aircraft missiles are missiles designed to shoot down aircraft. In that case no, perhaps it means abortion. Or maybe contraception and abortion, I'm not sure. I worked out that 'neo-natal' must mean 'successful births', and I headed that way in search of my child and its mother.

Getting into the maternity ward was easy; no-one challenged me as I strolled in through the reception area. I looked inside several smaller rooms but couldn't recognise anybody I even vaguely knew. After a few minutes of unsuccessful searching, I was accosted by a very young-looking Asian girl. She asked whether she could help me.

"Ah, hello," I replied. "I'm looking for Marian. She's just given birth – the baby's called Kimba."

"I'm sorry, sir," she replied, "but we don't have a baby Kimba right now. When was she born?"

"Yesterday, I assume. Or possibly the day before," I told her.

"You're not the father, are you, sir?" she asked.

"Marian certainly seems to think so," I replied. "'I know it must be from you' – that's what she wrote."

The nurse had referred to Kimba as 'she'. Up until that point, I hadn't considered the baby's sex, but I'd have said Kimba was short for Kimberley, a name which could be given to a boy or a girl. There was Kim Philby, the famous spy, and Kim Hughes, an Australian cricketer who 'Luvvie' Laithwaite often talks about. 'Luvvie' is Head of Drama, not sport, so why he's interested in cricketers is beyond me. I know why he's interested in spies: it's because many of them were homosexual, as most people know full well that he is.

"What's the mother's name?" the nurse asked me.

"Marian," I repeated.

"Surname?" she asked.

"Trumper," I replied, "Mister Peter Trumper."

"I meant the mother's surname," the nurse said. "If you'd like me to look her up in the records ...."

I explained that I didn't know her surname, I just knew her as Marian. The nurse couldn't think of a Marian among the new mothers, and since there wasn't a baby Kimba either, could I have come to the wrong hospital? That was possible, I had to admit.

I was impressed by how busy the staff were, all rushing about, yet this young lady had greeted me warmly and tried her best to help. All the other nurses too were smiling, smartly dressed and going happily about their tasks despite the strain they must be under. I felt this merited some reward, so I took out my card – the one I'd intended for Marian – and wrote a complimentary message to all NHS workers before handing it to the girl in reception on my way out.

I knew I couldn't phone round all the other hospitals in the area, especially without the key information of the mother's full name. I could wait for further news: when Kimba was allowed home, Marian might write to me again, perhaps with a photograph. But I couldn't be certain that she would.

However, one possibility remained. The postman had said that if I didn't pay for the letter, it would be returned to the sorting office where they'd try and trace the sender. Perhaps if I took the letter there myself, they'd be able to find her for me.

Fortunately, I know where the sorting office is. I sometimes go there to collect a parcel that the postman has been unable to deliver when I've been out. I took the letter with me and joined a queue at the counter. The clerk was a pale, weedy young man with a bored expression and the beginnings of a moustache on his upper lip. Finally, when he'd taken a card from each of the customers in front of me and slouched back from his storeroom with the appropriate package, my turn arrived.

"Good afternoon," I said. "I wonder if you could help me trace the person who sent me this letter."

"Is there a sender's address?" he asked. "Do you mind if I take a look?"

He inspected the envelope, then took out the letter and scrutinised that too. He even held it up to the light, as I had done, to see if an address had been written under the 'Fee to pay' sticker.

"When did you receive it?" he asked. I told him it was that morning.

"You had to pay a surcharge," he told me, as if I didn't already know. "The sender used the wrong stamp. Postage rates went up last year."

"Yes, I had to pay ten pounds. But the postman told me that if I didn't pay, the letter would be returned to sender." I thought of singing the chorus of *Return to Sender* by Elvis Presley, but decided not to. The clerk wouldn't appreciate my wit, and was probably too young to have heard of Elvis Presley.

"You shouldn't have paid ten pounds," he said. "£5.00 is the correct rate for an under-stamped letter. It's £10.00 if there's no stamp at all."

"I wasn't to know that," I objected. "The postman asked for ten pounds, and that's what I paid. Look, here's the receipt."

The young man asked to look at the envelope again. "It's very strange," he said, "but we haven't sold these stamps since last year, when the rates went up."

"Maybe whoever sent it was using up old stamps," I suggested, but the clerk scrutinised the envelope again and frowned.

"You see that franking mark?" he pointed out. "I know it's got a bit smudged, but we stopped using that frank over a year ago. The start of last year, it was."

"So, you're telling me this letter's been in the post for two years?" I was somewhat annoyed to reach this conclusion, and my voice showed it. It was the voice I use when a pupil gives me an implausible excuse for having failed to do his homework.

"I'd guess about eighteen months," he replied. "Judging by the code, it was probably posted around the September before last."

I was about to vent my rage still further, when he added, "Funny thing is, when your friend posted the letter, they put the correct stamp on it. It's just that the rates have gone up twice in the meantime."

I was now very angry. Sometimes as a teacher I pretend to be furious with a child who's earned my disapproval. But it's a false anger, intended to make the point that I'm the adult and can do or say whatever I like, whereas the child must do as I tell it. This time, though, I was truly livid.

"You mean to say I've been charged ten pounds to receive a letter, and all because it's taken you a year and a half to deliver it?" I raged. "I'll have you know that this letter contains vital information which I needed urgently eighteen months ago!"

"I'm very sorry, sir," the clerk offered. "You might want to fill in a complaint form. I'm sure once it was processed you'd qualify for a refund. That would probably take about three months."

"I don't care about the money," I roared, "I'm just disgusted by the appalling level of service. I shall expect a fulsome apology from the Postmaster General. He has my address, even if it takes him a year and a half to find it." And with that, I picked up the letter, the envelope and my receipt and stormed out of the sorting office.

That was why there was no sign of mother or baby in the maternity ward. My child was now eighteen months old! How could I start to build any relationship with it, or with its mother? I'd missed its first birthday and its first two Christmases, not to mention several stages in its development. By now, it would have said its first words, it could probably walk, and its personality should be starting to appear – its laughter, its energy, its joy when daddy walked into the room.

In the staffroom the following Monday, I was talking to 'Luvvie' Laithwaite, the Head of Drama. I get on well with him: I'm very tolerant of his camp theatricality which many of my colleagues simply pretend not to notice. I told him about my weekend's exploits at the hospital and the Post Office, berating the fact that I'd been charged ten pounds simply because my letter had been a year and a half in the post. I told him what was in the letter, and how my child must now be eighteen months old. I could say this with some pride – 'Luvvie' is never going to have children, whereas I could extol the joys of fatherhood. And I could say it without fear. If 'Luvvie' ever thought to make a scandal out of my having an illegitimate child that I've never seen, then I've certainly got enough dirt on him to end his teaching career!

'Luvvie' congratulated me on the new addition to my family and shared my concern that I had never seen my child.

"You've got to see her," he insisted. "Have you heard of Fathers for Justice? You should take it up with them."

I hadn't heard of Fathers for Justice, so he explained that it's a campaign group which promotes fathers' access rights to their children, supports them in the courts and lobbies parliament for changes to the law.

"But first you have to identify the mother," I pointed out, "and for the moment, I can't do that. I don't know who I'd be suing."

"And you've already tried the hospital and the post office to no avail," he mused. "What about an appeal in the paper? I'm seeing the reporter from The Gazette this afternoon – he's coming to do a piece about the school play, *Annie the Musical*. I could tell him about you."

"Would that help?" I wondered.

"Well, we could put out a piece – "Peter Trumper seeks contact with his lost daughter" – inviting the mother to get in touch. If she doesn't respond, then people who know her might."

"But I could get all kinds of cranks ringing me, claiming they can find her, asking me for money, just wasting my time," I objected.

"OK, here's what I suggest," he offered. "We issue an appeal, we ask Marian to get in touch. I'll give my phone number, and when anyone rings claiming to be Marian, I ask her the child's name, which we won't print in the article. If she knows it, then I ask for her surname and phone number, which I pass on to you. Then you can get back to anyone who sounds *bona fide*."

He was clearly trying to help, and I agreed to his idea.

"You know *Memphis Tennessee* by Chuck Berry?" he asked me.

I was about to say, "Of course I know it," but something about his tone suggested he might follow up with a question. "It's just slipped my mind for the moment," I said. "Remind me."

"It's about a man trying to get in touch with a girl," he explained. "But there's a clever bit of misdirection. At first you assume the girl must be his wife or partner, but then you realise that it's his daughter, who the mum has taken away from him."

"And does he manage to find her?" I asked.

"Well, no, but he asks the telephone company who it is that's been trying to contact him. That's the point of the song. It goes:

Long distance information, give me Memphis Tennessee,
Help me find the party trying to get in touch with me."

I was none the wiser, so he sang a couple more lines:

"*Help me, information, get in touch with my Marie,*
She's the only one who'd phone me here from Memphis Tennessee."

A couple of days later, the promised article appeared in The Gazette. I'd expected a small ad, but Luvvie had done even better: this was in the local news pages.

Schoolteacher seeks missing daughter

Local schoolteacher Peter Trumper is trying to contact Marian, the mother of his eighteen-month-old daughter. Mother and daughter have disappeared without trace but are believed to be living locally. A distraught Mr Trumper said, "I need to know that they're both OK. I'd be horrified if anything had happened to them. All I want is to have them back safely."

There was a number – Luvvie's – which anyone claiming to be Marian, or to know her whereabouts, could ring in confidence.

It was the end of the week before I caught up with Luvvie again. He didn't need to speak; his face alone told me that no-one had called. But he did say something that stopped me in my tracks.

"I've been thinking," he said, "Kimba's an odd name for a child. It's more of a dog's name. My neighbour's girl has a dog called Kimba. I'd always assumed she'd named it after *The Lion King*. You might remember her. Emma Chanderpaul – she left school the summer before last."

"Emma?"

"That's right. A sweet girl. Training to be a nurse. She really loves the dog – walks it twice a day, rain or shine. Even now, in the middle of February. Got it well trained, too."

"How old is it?"

"Young. Still quite puppyish. Maybe just over a year, a year and a half."

Of course I remembered Emma Chanderpaul, a quiet, polite girl who had never given me any trouble. She'd always wanted a dog, and her mother had promised her one if she passed her GCSEs and got a place at college. But at the final parents' evening before her daughter left school, Mrs Chanderpaul had told me she was worried: she naturally wanted Emma to do well and go to college, but as a single mother she simply could not afford to buy her daughter a dog.

I'd gone to the Animal Rescue Centre to see if they were giving any dogs away, as I've heard they often do. By chance, one of their rescue dogs had just given birth to a litter of puppies, which they were trying to get rid of. I gave Emma's address and asked them to deliver one of them to her as soon as it was ready to leave its mother. In what struck me as an act of brazen cheek, they asked me for a donation. Surely I was the one doing them a favour by taking an unwanted animal off their hands! Too astonished to give voice to my indignation, I'd handed over £20, the smallest note I happened to have in my wallet. I never heard any more about it, not a word, but all too quickly it was the start of a new school year and other things had taken priority.

I checked the records of former pupils in the school office. It was true that Emma had left the summer before last, and her mother's name was listed as Mrs Miriam Chanderpaul. Looking again at the signature on her letter to me, it could easily have been Miriam rather than Marian.

I decided not to contact her. She might have wondered why I'd not replied to her note at the time, but eighteen months had passed, which made it a bit awkward. I did worry, though, about what 'Luvvie' Laithwaite might tell people and how they'd react – "Mr Trumper thought he'd become a father, but he hadn't really; all that had happened was that a former pupil had got a dog." That might undermine my dignity.

I'm always very good at overcoming difficult situations, and I hoped I could find a solution here. The visit I arranged to France could have turned very nasty if it wasn't for my timely interventions. I'd secured glowing reports from Ofsted inspector George Roland and from John Crick in the 'critical friend' exercise. And everybody at school knew about my triumph on the BBC *Mastermind* programme, and the reason it had never been broadcast. What could I come up with now?

I returned to the Animal Rescue Centre and helped myself to one of their posters. No donation from me this time! Back at school, I was in the process of amending it when I was interrupted by Carol Jones, a junior member of my department. A pretty girl who studied at Cambridge, but her

French isn't a patch on mine, and she teaches her pupils absolutely nothing.

"Do I detect a happy event in the Trumper family? Or are you thinking of buying a dog?" she asked me.

"Certainly not," I retorted. "Perhaps you should get one, though. What about a French poodle – you might learn better French from it, *ha, ha, ha!*"

Instead of laughing, she just gave me the vacant expression she keeps for when I've said something too clever for her.

When I'd finished altering the poster, I stuck it on the staffroom noticeboard and stood back to admire my work. To the message that everyone should consider adopting a pet, I had added:

> Teachers (especially in the Drama department) who are likely to remain childless would do well to remember that a dog should never be seen as a replacement for a real infant.

My point made! Anyone reading it would assume it was Laithwaite who'd made the error. And I could assert that I knew all along about Emma's puppy, but Laithwaite had misinterpreted Mrs Chanderpaul's announcement of a 'new arrival in the family' with such hilarious results.

I always say that the reputation of the school is paramount. But since I'm so central to everything that happens there, then my reputation is equally paramount, if not more so. Once again, I'd done what was necessary to restore it, and I hoped that Luvvie's clumsy gaffe would 'dog' him, *ha, ha, ha!* for some time to come.

Just then, a voice behind me said, "Most interesting, Peter."

I turned round. It was Bryant, the headmaster, with a wry expression on his pompous old face.

I drew myself up to my full height. "Just a reminder to certain colleagues who might struggle to tell the difference between a baby and a dog," I smirked.

"Very appropriate," he commented. "And are you personally considering extending your pedigree?"

"Oh, no, headmaster, as a bachelor I don't see myself having a child in the immediate future," I assured him. I noticed Carol and Luvvie skulking near the lockers – I thought they'd both left the room.

"I wasn't just thinking of one," Bryant honked. "What about the rest of the litter? At £20 each, it would cost you £100, but I'm sure you could afford it."

He kept a straight face, but I could see Carol and Luvvie sniggering to one another in the corner.

"You'll have to excuse me, I've got a class to teach," I retorted as I turned and marched away.

Lightning Strikes

I'd just returned my trolley to the shelter after unloading my shopping. In thunder, lightning or in rain, is it really worth it just to get your pound coin back? Sometimes I don't bother; in my opinion a decent supermarket should employ a member of staff to do it for you. As I started the engine, a scruffy, dishevelled youth tapped at my steamed-up window. I opened it, knowing he'd be trying to cadge some money. I like to engage with these vagrants, reminding them that if they worked as hard as I do, then they'd be shopping at Waitrose, like me, instead of begging in the car park.

He pushed a piece of paper into my hand, which I took, knowing I'd throw it straight into the bin when I got home. But then he started muttering something, an incantation, maybe, or even a prayer. Not in English, or any other language that I could recognise. Middle Eastern, possibly.

"Aloo Achar!" he finished. Glancing down at the page he'd just given me, I recognised those same words printed near the bottom.

What I did next could have been fatal. I revved the engine and as drove as fast as I could to the far end of the car park. If he'd planted a bomb under me or chosen that moment to detonate his suicide vest, then I wouldn't be here to tell the tale.

From my mobile, I called 999. "Peter Trumper here," I said. "I'm in Waitrose car park. There's a potential terrorist." I described the man, adding that I could still see him approaching other drivers in search of his next victim.

The police called round later that evening. Constable Matthews introduced himself, and I invited him in. He'd have come to congratulate me on my bravery in the war against terror, of course, but I hoped Mrs Snoop from next door but one hadn't seen him. She might put an altogether different interpretation on my being visited by a uniformed police officer.

"You reported a suspicious individual," the constable reminded me. "You heard a phrase which you associated with extremism."

"That's right. Aloo Achar, or something like that."

"Do you know what that means, sir?" he asked.

"Literally, 'God is great,' I believe. But also 'I'm just about to blow us all up'."

The policeman shook his head. "He wasn't a terrorist," he said. "He was giving out flyers for an Indian restaurant."

"And his catchphrase?" I asked.

"Aloo Achar? Fried potatoes, spiced with peppers, chili and sesame. Delicious – you should try it, sir."

"Well, that's a relief, officer. But you can't be too careful nowadays."

"As a matter of fact, sir, you could be a bit more careful, and that's why I've called. Implying someone is a terrorist simply because of their ethnicity is an NCHI."

"A what?" I asked.

"A non-crime hate incident," the policeman explained. "Not a criminal offence as such, but we have to record occurrences in order to defuse community tensions."

"And what about defusing terrorist bombs?" I countered.

"Now, that's just my point. This isn't the first time we've spoken to you on this matter, is it, sir?"

"Really? What do you mean?"

From his briefcase, he took out an iPad, tapped the screen a few times, then read to me from the page he'd just opened. I'd always thought a policeman should take a pencil from behind his ear, lick it, then jot down his thoughts in a notebook. That's what PC Plod did in *Noddy and Big Ears*, if my memory is correct, and I can't see why that should change.

"A short while ago, you were spoken to by the police about racist, homophobic and antisemitic comments made in a café," he explained. "You claimed to have been having tea and cakes with Victor Hugo, the 19th century French novelist."

"It was Marcel Proust, actually," I corrected him.

"Yes, sir, I'm sure it was. That's why we took no further action at the time – we assumed you were, shall we say, misguided, sir."

"It's you that's misguided. Fancy not knowing your Proust from your Victor Hugo!"

"Can I ask you, sir, do you feel well in yourself?"

"Perfectly," I retorted.

"I'm not a medical man," the policeman admitted, "but agitation, delusions, that can indicate a stress-related illness. And you do look pale and restless. Sir, we'd be prepared to take this no further if you had a check-up with your doctor. Here's my phone number at the station – let me know when you've arranged to do that."

I wouldn't normally do something simply because I was told to. But there was something in the policeman's manner that made me think he was trying to be helpful rather than authoritarian. And

I do have a stressful job – not only do I have my own classes to teach, but I have everyone else's work to do too! The school's administration is a nightmare, the headmaster has no idea what he's doing, and it's up to me to tell my junior colleagues not only what to teach but also how.

It wasn't the doctor who saw me, but his practice nurse. A pretty girl with a charming manner and full of useful advice. I had some wise counsel for her too – a shorter skirt, a bit more cleavage, think of the nurses in the old *Carry On* films – which she gratefully acknowledged. But she wanted to reduce my blood pressure, not send it even higher, she said!

As well as high blood pressure, she told me my sugar level was somewhere up in the stratosphere. Cholesterol was an issue too: I was on the verge of diabetes. I told her I drank very little and had never smoked, but she was more interested in what I ate.

"Only healthy meals," I assured her.

"What did you have yesterday?" she asked.

I tried to remember. I know it was very good – my charlady, Mrs Lee, cooks me a set of meals twice a week which I keep in the fridge or freezer until I need them.

"Shepherd's pie," I finally decided.

"Any vegetables?"

"Yes, chips. From the microwave."

"A dessert? Some fruit, perhaps?"

"Dessert, yes. Rice pudding – always my favourite. That or bread and butter pudding. Must be made with real cream. Then you add jam and sugar, although some people prefer honey."

"That was in the evening, I take it. What about lunchtime?"

"I always go to the school canteen. A bacon sandwich. Sometimes a pizza. Or both. A cream doughnut. A coffee. Perhaps I ought to cut down on the coffee?" I suggested.

"Mr Trumper, when did you last eat something green?"

"Green? Oh, never. That would mean it had gone mouldy. I wouldn't eat anything which had gone off. Very bad for you."

By 'something green,' she meant salads and vegetables, apparently. She then asked me about exercise. I told her I'd recently played football for the staff against the pupils and been the 'Man of the Match.' She asked me if I played every week, and I realised it was in fact two years since that game. Odd that I wasn't invited to play last year!

"Apart from the tablets I'm going to prescribe," she told me, "You need to change your diet and get some regular exercise. What you need is an allotment."

"You mean a little garden?" I said. "That's not for me. That's an old person's hobby."

"Not at all," she argued. "My father has one – he's around your age. I know there are some vacant plots, and they're not expensive to rent. He grows his own vegetables, and the exercise does him a world of good – digging, hoeing – plus the open air, of course."

I don't know how old she thought I was. If she was 25, her father must be around 50, and I'd always associated allotment gardening with retired people. My date of birth must be on her records, so I hadn't claimed to be in my early thirties, which is what I usually tell people, but if she looked at me and thought I was in my fifties, well, that's an insult. But perhaps she had a point, and I did need to modify my way of life.

And so, I became a tenant farmer, with my own allotment garden. I'd have liked a title to come with my estate, so that I could call myself Lord Trumper of the Manor, but that's for another day. It's about a mile from my home, 10 by 20 yards of good, fertile soil, surrounded by other similar smallholdings.

Word soon spread at school, and people commented. Old Bryant, the headmaster, said to me one morning after assembly, "As Voltaire once wrote, '*Il faut cultiver notre jardin*'." Others said something similar, although no one bothered to tell me who Voltaire is. Not as though I'd be interested!

As a superb speaker of French, I know that the hallmark of a great linguist is his use of the subjunctive. Bryant and the rest had simply said, "*Il faut cultiver………*" which is an infinitive. I decided to tell the next person to say it that the correct expression should be, "*Il faut que nous ………*" and then the subjunctive of *cultiver*. I looked it up; it's *cultivions*, apparently. I'd tell everyone I'd known it all along.

I soon realised an allotment is hard work, and too time consuming for a busy man like me. Tom, one of the other tenants (or was he called Ted, or Terry?) offered to tend my plot every week, plant me a healthy selection of salads, fruits and vegetables, pick them and deliver them to my door. I took him up on that, and we agreed a suitable payment. Most smallholders prefer to do their own spadework, as they call it, but they're not from the hard-working *bourgeoisie*.

Once I was spared the manual labour, I spent some happy times on my allotment. I chatted to Tom as he went about his work, and to some of the other gardeners too. I supervised their efforts and was able to put my management skills to good use.

There's a bucolic air to the place, and I'm sure the weather is sunnier and the sky bluer than in other parts of town! My neighbours were simple folk, without pretentions to intellect or education, and I know they admired me for my professional status. They had unhappy memories of their own schooldays, but were pleased to have found a vocation which allowed them to till the earth, take pride in their produce, and enjoy the company of their fellows. I learnt some interesting things too: with their knowledge and enthusiasm, they told me all about the best time to plant, how to eliminate pests, and when to harvest. Perhaps some of their wisdom could be applied to nurturing children – after all, most of my pupils probably have the same IQ as one of their courgettes.

On one of my visits, I decided I needed to add a greenhouse. I'd heard that tomatoes, peppers and even grapes would benefit from hothouse conditions. Imagine it – I could be making my own wine! *Château Trumper*, indeed! I went to an upmarket garden centre and instructed them to supply, deliver and erect their best greenhouse on my estate. Not one of the popular chains, you'll note, and not a cheap greenhouse either; the salesman explained that this one had shatterproof glass and many other special features. As for the cost, the price I admitted paying depended on who I was telling the story to.

Tom (I think I've got his name right) told me that greenhouses were forbidden on the allotments, although a few other tenants had them. Greenhouse glass can crack in hot weather, and owners don't always clear away the fragments which then cause injury to people and wildlife. Storms, vandalism and neglect don't help, either. But surely that didn't apply to my expensive, tempered safety glass! Why should I be forced to follow regulations that are clearly intended for the poorer people, the ignorant and less educated gardeners?

It's the same at school. There are rules which the pupils must obey, because they can't be trusted to think for themselves. The correct uniform; one staircase going up, another for coming down, and a one-way system on the corridors. Orderly queuing in the canteen. Those rules don't apply to us, of course: we teachers dress how we choose, find our own way around the building, and are entitled to jump to the front of the dinner queue. That's only fair.

Back to my greenhouse. The Town Council served me a notice instructing me to dismantle it. I don't know how they found out – a mole must have tipped them off, and by that I mean a treacherous informant, not a burrowing rodent, *ha, ha, ha!* But one thing I do know is that you need to talk to councillors like you do to schoolchildren, and that's something I'm very good at. Astonishingly, they refused to accept my point of view. It was the same rule for everybody, they insisted. And that clearly isn't right!

Ted (that's the man's name, not Tom, now I think of it) said that he, like several other growers, was a member of the National Allotment Society. He suggested writing to them. I did, and an inspector visited me. The inspector complimented me on how tidily I kept my plot. He even quoted *"Il faut cultiver notre jardin,"* to which I replied that to be correct, he ought to use a subjunctive and say, *"Il faut que nous cultivions notre jardin."* He didn't thank me – I wonder whether he'd even heard of Voltaire – but more importantly, he agreed that my greenhouse truly was a superior one, and the glass met the highest possible standards. But the National Allotment Society couldn't challenge the local council, which was legally entitled to enforce its own rules.

But do you know who is the patron of the National Allotment Society? Here's a clue: he's a keen gardener himself, although I imagine he has more staff than I do. You've guessed? It's Prince Charles, the Prince of Wales. I wrote to him at Buckingham Palace, confident that he'd support me in my campaign against the petty bureaucrats. One of his lackeys wrote back, saying that protocol prevented His Royal Highness from taking sides in any dispute. How ridiculous! Honestly, I don't think that man could ever become King! Imagine if Queen Elizabeth the First had refused to take sides against the Spanish Armada, or Winston Churchill had declared he was neutral in World War Two! That's not what I'd call leadership!

I was proved right, as I always am, when another bout of lightning storms struck the town. Trees were uprooted, and there was extensive flooding. At the allotments, many potting sheds and greenhouses were destroyed, and others badly damaged. And whose superior quality greenhouse survived fully intact? Yes, mine!

And then, something happened which amused me very much. The owners of damaged buildings received letters from the council saying they had to either clear away all debris or else rebuild the structure, making it fully safe. I made several visits to my allotment, asking my fellow owners how much repairs were costing them, and reminding them that I'd avoided all that effort and expense by opting for a quality model in the first place. As a fluent German speaker, I was able to say *"Scheißenfreude"* to them – that means "Your problem, not mine," I believe.

Even funnier was an event of a few months later. By now, everybody who had a shed or greenhouse had complied with the council's order to rebuild it. But then came a series of rail strikes. Short, unannounced, but calculated to have the maximum impact on travellers and the general public. 'Lightning strikes,' they call them. I wasn't affected – I never travel by rail – but after a protest meeting at the station, a group of angry train drivers rampaged through the town causing widespread damage and injury. I don't know why anyone trusts these individuals with a train – I wouldn't put one of them in charge of a pram! – and I know they're already very well paid for the simple job they do. Of course, the trades unions denied that their men were involved in the rioting, preferring to blame hangers-on and opportunists, but once again there was carnage at the allotments. And again, my greenhouse survived when others had their windows smashed or were burnt down.

I was at the allotments one Saturday, surveying the scene and trying to remember who it was that had written, "*Il faut cultiver notre jardin.*" I used the phrase several times: many feeble and inferior greenhouses and other outbuildings once again had to be demolished and re-built from scratch, and the land around them cleared and re-dug. I gloated in the knowledge that mine had again survived unscathed, which surely justified my having invested in quality at the outset.

Suddenly, a great roar surrounded us. Two military aeroplanes shot overhead, so low that they almost skimmed the rooftops, and we could clearly see the pilots inside them. They circled, gathering pace so that smoke billowed out behind them. As they screeched above us for a second time, they both stood up on end and rose like rockets into the sky, flames erupting from the backs of their engines. There were two mighty booms. I found out later that the first one was the crash of them breaking through the sound barrier as they powered away from us. As for the second, that was obvious as we looked around: it was every pane of glass we could see shattering into a million pieces. This time, my greenhouse was not exempt. A heap of fragmented glass and twisted metal lay where it had stood just seconds earlier.

Ted (or was he called Terry?) told me afterwards that the two aeroplanes were called F35 Lightnings. They were *en route* from their base in Norfolk to a low-flying training exercise over the Lake District, when suddenly they were diverted to intercept a Russian bomber which had illegally entered British airspace. So, we'd had three lightning strikes at the allotments: the storm, the train drivers and now the aeroplanes. The one saving grace was that the other gardeners couldn't glory in my misfortune, since they'd all suffered equally from the third strike, as well as having borne the consequences of the first two.

To make matters worse, my insurance company refused to pay out compensation. Their excuse was that the greenhouse was an unauthorised structure, therefore not covered against loss or damage. That hadn't stopped them charging me the premiums, though!

I've now given up my allotment garden. Trevor took it over from me. That's his name, I think, although I keep calling him Ted or Terry, which might be a mistake. He got rid of all the fragments of my shattered greenhouse, so there won't ever be a vintage *Château Trumper*, but he still delivers me a parcel of fresh fruit and vegetables every week when they're in season, for which I pay him a reasonable price. Much cheaper than buying them at Waitrose, and without the hassle of having to do it all myself!

I don't care who it was that said, "*Il faut cultiver notre jardin.*" Not only did he fail to use a French subjunctive, but he was factually wrong. Because we don't have to cultivate our gardens. Much easier is to pay someone else to do it for us.

Shortly after the final Lightning strike and passing my allotment over to Trevor, I took 'Luvvie' Laithwaite, the Head of Drama, out for a meal. I'd got into a slightly embarrassing situation over a dog, which he happened to know rather too much about, even though it was none of his business. Treating him to dinner would be a good way of ensuring his silence, I thought.

We went to the Golden Poppadom in Market Street and ate well. No need to recount everything we selected from the extensive menu, but we did choose Aloo Achar which, as everybody knows, is fried potato spiced with peppers, chili and sesame. I thought I recognised our waiter, and after a few minutes I realised he was none other than the young man I'd first seen distributing flyers in the Waitrose car park. Out of the storm, and spruced up in traditional Indian kurta and churidar, he looked very smart indeed.

I don't know whether he recognised me or not. "Beware of Aloo Achar," he warned us. "Taste is very fiery. You will think a bomb is exploding in your mouth!"

"I'm not sure about a bomb," 'Luvvie' said when he'd eaten his portion. "More like a bolt of lightning, I'd have said."

Explosion or lightning strike, Aloo Achar was every bit as delicious as PC Matthews had promised me it would be.

My Sentimental Education

My next-door neighbour in Church View is a strange man. When I first bought my house, I thought he was called Mr Laurel, like Stan Laurel of Laurel and Hardy, but he's not. He's called Mr Laurels. As in two laurels, plural, more than one.

Perhaps to stop people calling him Mr Laurel, or even Stanley by mistake, he planted two laurel trees in his front garden when he first moved in. That was when the houses were new, around fifteen years ago. Since his first name is Charles, I sometimes call him Charles of the Laurels – a bit like Tess of the D'Urbervilles. That's a play by William Shakespeare, which I know very well, of course.

The laurels have grown quite tall now, although he does keep them neatly clipped.

"I see you're trimming your bush again, Mr Laurel," I say to him when I see him doing exactly that. I have a reputation for sparkling repartee, as everybody knows. One day I hope to see him fall off his ladder, and I'll say: "Here's another fine mess you've gotten into, Stanley!" but that's not happened yet.

More often, though, I see him washing his old Honda. He does that every Saturday morning, and I always say to him, "I expect you'll do mine next, *ha, ha, ha!*" One day he'll give my cutting-edge quip the acknowledgement it truly deserves.

I was arriving home one Saturday lunchtime, just as Mrs Lee, my cleaner, was leaving. I'd been to the shops and was hoping she'd be able to unload my car boot and put all the shopping into my cupboards, but Mr Laurels kept me talking. In fact, I think he was stalling and waiting for her to go, because once the coast was clear, he leaned towards me in a conspiratorial sort of way and whispered, "I say, Trumper old chap, what do you like to do for a bit of fun on a weekend?"

I thought that was a rather personal question, but I considered it and gave my answer. "I spend quite a lot of time marking my pupils' homework," I told him. "I quite enjoy that, and then I like to ensure my lessons are all prepared for the week ahead."

"That's not what I meant," he hissed, "I mean for entertainment? You know, company?"

I defended my answer. "I find it entertaining to mark my pupils' work," I explained. "Often, they make amusing mistakes which I can have a good laugh about. And I like to rehearse the witty remarks I can spontaneously use in my lessons."

I didn't add that on Saturday evenings I also like to watch a romantic comedy on DVD – I've got quite a collection, many of them featuring Hugh Grant, who looked rather like me in his younger days. Or better still, one of the old *Carry On* films from the 1970s with Barbara Windsor and all those other great actors and actresses of the period.

But marking homework clearly wasn't the answer he wanted, and before his next question he looked furtively up and down the street to check that Mrs Lee had indeed gone and that no-one else had strayed within earshot.

"All right," he said, "Supposing you were married, and your wife was away visiting her sister for the weekend. You know what they say, 'While the cat's away!' What would you do then?"

"I certainly wouldn't spend time washing my car," I answered, "But if you're at a loss for something to do, you could always clean mine, *ha, ha, ha!*" As ever, he failed to chortle at my impromptu wit.

"I thought we could go to the football, you and me" he said. It wasn't a suggestion; he sounded as though he'd already made up his mind. "Your lad's playing – Tony Caldwell, our number 6. He went to your school, didn't he?"

I vaguely remembered the name. There was a Caldwell in my A-Level French class a few years ago; no great talent, I seemed to recall.

"They say he'll play for England one day," Laurels went on. "He'll have to move to a bigger club first, mind you. Anyway, I've got us a couple of tickets. Then we could go on to a party that a certain lady-friend of mine is having at 'you know where'."

"Wouldn't that look a bit strange, two men arriving together at a party?" I asked. "Are you sure you wouldn't rather take someone else?" I hadn't really got all that much schoolwork to do, and I was rather looking forward to a date that evening with Hattie Jacques in *Carry On Matron*.

"Not at all," he reassured me, "Lots of other men go, either on their own or in a group. There'll be plenty of ladies, too – you'll enjoy it."

"Odd that your lady-friend is throwing a party on the very weekend your wife happens to be away," I said, but he assured me she had one every weekend, and on several weekdays too.

We arranged to meet after lunch. I went in, not relishing the thought of unpacking and putting all my shopping away myself, but I managed it. Mrs Lee had made me a rather tasty soup, and I'd bought a crusty loaf at the baker's – it was one of the items on the list she'd given me. What I hadn't told her was that I'd also been to the chemists to pick up my new prescription; I'd been feeling a bit short of breath and had visited the doctor earlier in the week. I knew I had high blood pressure – mine is a stressful and responsible job, after all, and I'm also taking tablets for blood sugar and cholesterol. But shortness of breath was something new, and I now had another set of tablets. As I was to take two with every meal, I took four: two to accompany my lunch, and two in anticipation of the tea-time meal I'd be missing since a football match and a party might stretch on into the early evening. Perhaps I'd have a late supper if I was home around 8.

Before going out again, I thought about getting changed, but decided against it; a football match would be outdoors, and the spring weather hadn't arrived yet. I'd need to keep warm, so I put on my thick woollen overcoat and a bright cashmere scarf. I slipped the packet of pills into my pocket in case I wasn't home by the time I expected to be.

Laurels sent me back inside when he saw my scarf. "Not yellow," he insisted, "Yellow's Norwich colours – they're the opposition! Unless of course you're channelling Oscar Wilde," he added.

He probably thought I hadn't heard of Oscar Wilde, but I have. I was able to strike back: "No, you're wrong. Oscar Wilde was Irish. So he'd be wearing green, not yellow." But so as not to be confused with a player from the other team, I swapped my scarf for a similar one in pillar box red.

I'd never previously attended a football match. Not for lack of time; it's simply that I've never been interested. I couldn't tell you how to get to the football ground because it's somewhere I'd never go. I was pleased that Laurels drove. Otherwise, I'd have been worried about leaving my BMW cabriolet in what I assumed would be a working class area of town, where it might attract the wrong kind of attention. Laurels not only knew the way but found a good parking spot. From there, you could see the grandstands and quite a lot of people, many of them dressed in football colours, all heading in the same direction.

Inside the stadium, I noted that every spectator had a seat – a cheap, folding plastic one, but more than I expected. I really thought spectators at football matches stood up – wasn't that why it was named 'the stand?' I could see at the far end all the opposition supporters had been corralled together, and that area was a mass of yellow. Our section of the arena was less crowded and there were several empty seats, but the supporters' chanting gave the place an intimidating atmosphere. Much of it was obscene, and I'd have felt quite vulnerable if I'd been wearing the opposition's colours. Mr Laurels had done well to warn me on that score.

Once the game started, I became increasingly aware of how long it was taking either side to score a goal. The crowd – which had swelled considerably in the moments before kick-off – sensed it too, and there were groans and slow handclapping. I don't think any goals had been scored by either side after three quarters of an hour, unless one or two had happened when I wasn't paying attention, but I think I'd have noticed. When the referee blew his whistle and the players all came to a halt, there was more booing and most of the crowd stood up as if to leave. I was ready to do the same.

"Where are you going?" Laurels asked me.

"Isn't that it?" I asked, "That's the end, isn't it?"

He explained that there was another forty-five minutes of the same still to go, but he was paying a quick visit to the lavatory and would come back with something for us both. I guessed it might be food, since there was a pungent smell of warm fat and fried onions – worse than in the school canteen, I thought, even though we were outdoors. Fortunately, it wasn't too cold, and people were coming and going all around me.

"Is this your first match?" a man in the next seat but one asked me.

"Oh no," I replied, "I often go to football matches, but I've never been to one here."

"I thought not," he said. "We sometimes see Charlie here, not often, just when his wife's away, but I didn't think I'd seen you before."

"Who do you support, then?" his companion asked me.

I couldn't name many football teams, but I knew that saying the wrong thing can lead to trouble in such a situation, so I tried to project my schoolmaster's wisdom and authority into my answer.

"I support the individual who has talent and flair," I said, "The man whose exceptional skill marks him out as the best at what he does."

"You'll not get that here," another supporter mockingly joined in. "That type of player, you're talking about fifty million plus. City, Liverpool, Arsenal, they pay that, but we can't afford that kind of money."

"Caldwell's the best of our bunch," the first man added. "A local lad, but he'll not stay long. I just hope we get a good price for him."

"Well, I suppose the top people do deserve the top salaries," I pointed out. That doesn't apply in my profession, mind you – I'm paid just the same as the Head of Science, the Head of English and even the Head of Sport, although I clearly have ten times their ability.

"See, we play different from your top sides," a different voice chimed in, "We have to. Without your Ronaldos and your Messis, we play as a team. Defend in numbers, attack in numbers. It might not be pretty, but it works."

"But I still prefer the man who's a cut above the rest," I argued. "The role model, the one they all look up to. A bit like myself in my own profession."

Our discussion went no further as Laurels returned carrying a paper bag, from which he took two meat pies and handed one to me. Before taking a bite of his own, he reached inside his puffer jacket and produced two bottles of beer, removing the caps with an opener taken from his trouser pocket. Again, one was intended for me. He apparently expected me to eat the pie and drink the beer with not a plate, knife, fork or glass in sight! And in public too!

"Just one thing," he said, "Try and keep the bottle out of view. Officially, there's no drinking within sight of the pitch."

His technique was to wolf the pie as if he hadn't eaten for days, and to make short work of the beer by putting the bottle directly to his lips. I ate and drank as much as I could before slipping what I couldn't finish under my seat. I accompanied this impromptu snack with a couple more tablets; after all, the instructions clearly stated I was to take two with every meal, and I washed them down with a mouthful of the gassy beer.

The game resumed, in much the same style as before, although I could tell the teams had changed ends. This time, the noise of the crowd grew louder as play approached our end of the pitch, and the yellow-clad fans at the far end became more excited as the cluster of players shuffled in their direction. The referee seemed to have more to do, blowing his whistle and pointing randomly at individual players, and this usually resulted in a chorus of obscenities from the crowd.

Finally, the match was over, and the players trooped off. I didn't want to embarrass myself by asking who had won, so I suppose I'll never know. As we filed out of the stadium and back towards Laurels' car, I did have some questions, though.

"You knew the match was going to be against Norwich," I said, "even before we left Church View. You warned me not to wear a yellow scarf. Does our team play against Norwich every week? It's a long way for them to come."

He laughed and said everybody knew. The newspapers print the 'fixtures,' as he called them, at the start of every season. A fan who goes to every home match will see every other team in the division.

"Those supporters sitting near us," I asked, "Do you know them?"

"Not all that well," he replied, "I see them when I'm able to get to a match, which isn't as often as I'd like."

"Are they very working class?" I wondered.

"I wouldn't say so. Next to me, he's a software developer. A couple of them are sales managers, there's a graphic designer, some businesspeople. Why do you ask?"

"I thought some of them had very ignorant opinions. They seemed to prefer mediocrity over talent, and were proud that their team played that way."

"I'm sure that's not what they meant," he argued. "No, football's moved away from the working class. The ticket prices have seen to that! You just couldn't afford to go every week if you were a factory hand or a shop assistant."

"Then how do you explain all the shouting and swearing?" I asked.

"People care about their football," he replied. "Win or lose, it means a lot to them. I take it you weren't impressed. Let's drown our sorrows before we head on."

We were passing a pub whose main door opened straight onto the street, and Laurels shepherded me inside. The low, dimly lit saloon was no bigger than the front room of a terraced house. There were a couple of rustic tables, but most customers were standing, including the cluster of men around the bar who greeted Laurels into their midst. To say the room was so full, it seemed eerily quiet. The air was dense and cloudy; I knew smoking had been banned in pubs a few years ago, but the stench of tobacco still lingered. Perhaps there was a side room where it still went on.

Without either of us having ordered, two pints of brown beer were placed in front of us, and Laurels raised one of them to me.

"Cheers!" he called, and took a deep draught, whilst I sipped at mine. It was warm, harsh and unpleasant. If I'd had the opportunity to look at the wine list, I'd have chosen a glass of *Pinot Grigio*.

Laurels introduced me to his friends. "This is my neighbour, Peter," he said, "He's a schoolteacher." He went on to introduce the others, but so quickly that I couldn't fully take in the names. There was Prince Harry (who was really called Harry Prince), Donkey Dave, Narky Nick; the names flew past me and I may have got them all wrong. I shared with them my nickname for my neighbour: Charles of the Laurels. I wish now I'd had longer to prepare, and then I might have treated them to my quip about him always trimming his bush.

One of them asked me which subject I taught. I think he was impressed, since very few adults have any ability in a foreign language, and even other teachers lack my true mastery. I often tell people I don't enjoy rubbing shoulders with the riffraff at parents' evenings, but the fact is I do; humble parents consult me just as ignorant patients might consult their GP, and I confidently dispense my wisdom and judgement. "I don't think there's a serious problem, Mr and Mrs Thompson; just make sure your daughter keeps following my instructions and everything will sort itself out," is a reassuring line that anxious parents might hear either from a doctor or from myself.

This conversation, however, took a different turn. They all wanted to brag about their own children – one was a regular for his school's football team; another had just been put into the top set for maths; a third liked his science teacher but wasn't strong in geography. As if I cared! Not knowing the children concerned, I could neither instruct nor advise, and the conversation slipped away from me.

But when they reminisced over their own schooldays and wondered whether exams had got easier or harder, my expertise rose once again to the fore.

"Much easier," I informed them. "When I did my school exams, it was very difficult to get a top grade, and I was one of very few students to do so. Nowadays, over 50% end up with Grade A or B."

"You say that," one of them tried to argue, "but I'm an accountant, and I can't do half the stuff my 14-year-old comes home with in Maths. It's a different world from our day."

"A lot more pressure too," someone else put in. "When we left school, there were plenty of jobs. Now they've no chance unless they've got top grades and been to college and university."

"But getting to university is so much easier," I explained. "Over half of today's school leavers are given places. When I left school, only the top ten percent of us went to university." I withheld the fact that the ten percent didn't include me – I went to the Technical College when I was already into my twenties.

"But is it worth going to university?" Laurels asked. "I mean, students now, what with fees and living costs, they finish up with a whole load of debts. That's no way to start your working life."

"Of course it's worth it," I maintained. "A degree opens all kinds of doors. It's the gateway to the lifestyle everyone aspires to."

"I disagree," one of them was bold enough to assert. No wonder they all called him Donkey Dave – he was positively asinine in his opinions.

"Medicine, Law, maybe some of the sciences, but what good is an arts degree? English, History, Sociology – I bet ninety percent of them end up as schoolteachers."

"What we need," declared the one I think was known as Prince Harry, "is proper apprenticeships. Train the kids for the jobs that are out there. We're short of plumbers, nurses, electricians, builders. So, what do we do? We end up bringing in migrants. Someone needs to put two and two together."

"That's true," I conceded, "And there ought to be a glut of people queuing up to service the needs of we, the professional classes. I know how hard it is to find a gardener or a painter and decorator."

"In my view," Laurels asserted, "the whole structure needs to be pulled down. University's for privileged kids who grow up into privileged adults. Which school you went to, whether your parents can pay, that's what gets you into university. I'd scrap them all."

"But you're middle class," I told him. "You're a civil servant and you live in Church View. How can you object to the system that keeps everyone in their proper place?"

"I'm not as middle class as you," Laurels replied. "I started out as a clerical assistant – that's the lowest grade there is. No graduate entry scheme for me. My dad was a labourer. Yours owned his own business – I bet that opened doors for you."

"That's only normal," I countered. "Yes, he gave me my first job when I left school, in charge of his sales department. But what father wouldn't do that for his only son?"

"One who wasn't the MD of his own company, that's who," one of Laurels' companions retorted.

"And besides," I added, "he sold his company when he retired. What the Trumper family has now is the product of hard work, not privilege. Anyone starting out in life need only follow my example of talent and industry."

Rather than prolong the debate, Laurels urged me to "Drink up!" I think he was angling for a second pint, but I was feeling bloated, remembering that I'd already drunk most of the bottle that he'd given me at the match. I wondered too whether the pills I'd taken were beginning to have an effect. Was I supposed to avoid alcohol, perhaps? He finally took the hint that I'd had enough, and we left our companions and headed back to where he'd parked his car.

"What a dull set of people," I told him, "All they wanted to talk about was themselves and their own stupid opinions."

"Not your type?" he correctly deduced. "Never mind, you'll enjoy where we're going next."

He was a touch secretive as we got in the car, but he seemed to know where he was heading. It was variously known as 'you know where,' 'a certain street,' or 'down by the bridge,' he told me.

"You said a party," I reminded him. "With ladies present."

"You could call them ladies," he cryptically replied.

"Not transvestites, I hope?"

"No, no, definitely of a female persuasion," he assured me. "But not so ladylike in their behaviour, thank goodness! That reminds me ...." Reaching across, he passed me an envelope from the glove box which he said I was to present to our hostess before we left.

"Perhaps we should take our ladies some flowers?" I suggested.

"And where would we get flowers now all the shops are shut?" he asked. "Last time you took a lady flowers, where did you get them?

I tried to think back. "Actually, it was from my parents' garden," I said. "I was 14. My mother had set me up on a date with a neighbour's daughter. She picked me a bunch of tulips to take to her house."

"And did they do the trick?" he enquired.

"Not exactly. I wasn't sure what to do, so I ended up giving them to the mother and not the daughter," I explained.

"Didn't you fancy her?" he asked me.

"Not really. She wasn't what you'd call attractive," I explained. "14, that's just the age you start to notice these things. In fact, her mother was the better-looking of the two. Married, unfortunately."

"Women with 14-year-old daughters often are," Laurels said. "Doesn't always stop them, though. Have you seen her since?"

"I sometimes see the daughter when I visit my parents," I admitted.

"Do you ever speak to her?"

"A couple of times, I have. The last time, she said she spent ten years hoping to be asked for a second date. Then her mum died, and she had to become a full-time carer for her dad."

"And in ten years, you never gave her a second thought?" Laurels queried.

"I travelled, I came home, I saw the world, I had other loves," I lied.

"The one that got away, then. But you can do better. The nearest place that sells flowers this time of night is the petrol station on Moor Lane. We'll make a detour, if it makes you feel happier."

I bought two bunches of flowers, and we drove on. It was quite dark by now, but I knew we were on the outskirts of town, near the river. The old houses were large, stone rather than brick, some in darkness but many with lights in the windows. We stopped in front of one of them. On a windowsill stood a bowl of goldfish and a reseda in a flowerpot. The glow of the porchlight also revealed a woman wearing brash make up, a short white dress, and long, dangling earrings. When we drew nearer, I could see that she had a foreign complexion, Middle Eastern perhaps.

"Zora's Turkish," Laurels whispered to me, "Be careful what you say."

"Ah, Mister Laurels," the woman greeted us as we approached the house, "long time I not see you. Welcome back. You have brought friend?"

"Yes, a friend," he replied, "It's his first visit. This is my neighbour and very good friend Peter Trumper. He's a schoolteacher."

"A Head of Department, actually," I clarified, as I should have done when Laurels introduced me to his friends in the pub. "Peter Trumper, *professeur de français. Enchanté, Madame.*"

"Your friend is my friend too," she simpered, "I am sure we have good girl for him. You bring flowers for me, or for your girl?"

I offered her one of the bunches of flowers. She seemed pleased and led us from the porch into a hallway and then to an empty parlour where the heat and the smell of perfume were quite overwhelming. She invited us to sit down – the two of us side-by-side on a chintz sofa – and then left, returning shortly afterwards carrying a tray with two glasses of sparkling wine.

"Some champagne while you wait," she explained.

We each took a glass, clinked them together, and took a sip. Left alone once more, we had time to finish almost the whole glass. I looked at Laurels and said, "Strange that we seem to be the only guests."

"Give it a moment," he replied.

Our hostess reappeared, followed by two girls. Aged around twenty, both were of foreign appearance, one African, the other much paler, Eastern European, perhaps. The darker one wore only underwear, topped with a lacy sort of shroud; the pale one was dressed as a comedy schoolgirl – she could have been from one of my *Carry On* films – with an indecently short skirt, a white blouse and a striped tie.

"MCC," Laurels whispered to me, and when I looked at him blankly, he explained, "The tie – red and yellow. Bacon and egg."

I'm afraid the explanation meant even less to me than the initials. It looked like a school tie to me, although I couldn't place it as belonging to any local school. I wondered whether the outfit – or the girl – had anything to do with Laurels announcing my profession to Madame Zora.

I thrust my remaining bunch of flowers towards the darker girl. Favouring white over black might be seen as racist, something I certainly wanted to avoid. And I didn't want to encourage the one who reminded me of the perils that lie in store for unwary schoolteachers. She thanked me and gave me a peck on the cheek, which was unexpected but not unpleasant.

But the pale girl moved closer, and her hand brushed my lapel. I smelt her perfume – musk and other heavy spices – and felt myself stiffen. Her fingers slipped down, and she started to undo the top button of my overcoat.

"*Tu n'as pas chaud, mon chéri?*" she asked.

"Oh – er ……… *oui, oui, oui, c'est vrai, je suis très, très chaud,*" I agreed. It wasn't just the heat; the fear of the unknown and even the choice I'd had to make were pressing down on me. The pie I'd eaten, the beer and wine I'd drunk and the tablets too, all added to my nausea, and I felt my spirit drain. I stood quite still – maybe I should have visited the lavatory during the football game as Laurels had done. But when I answered the schoolgirl's French with a fluent phrase of my own, the two girls laughed. Zora smiled too, and I sensed the three of them conspiring to mock my embarrassment. As I reeled back, they must have noticed that I could no longer contain my pleasure.

I knocked against a small table, dislodging a lamp which I was just able to steady with my hand as I strained to keep my balance.

And then came a flash of inspiration. I cried: "Here's another fine mess you've gotten us into, Stanley!"

I'd waited a long time to deliver that line!

Strangely, though, instead of laughing louder, the ladies fell silent and looked aghast. I summoned my remaining strength and staggered to the door. Laurels called me to return, but since I still had the envelope for Madame Zora, he had to follow me back to the car.

As we were leaving we passed a man I recognised as the father of one of my pupils. I presume he would have recognised me too: at a recent parents' evening, he'd had the nerve to accuse me of not marking his child's homework – homework which, I informed him quite bluntly, the child had failed to do. We crossed without acknowledging one another.

The following Saturday, Laurels was again out washing his car as I was coming home with my groceries. "No match this week – they're playing away," he informed me. I took that to mean we also wouldn't be repeating our other visits of the previous weekend. He looked round to check that his wife wasn't within earshot, and said to me:

"Still, we had a good time, didn't we?"

"Yes, very good," I replied. "Perhaps another day ……." but I let my thoughts tail away.

It had been a good day; one of my best, even. I'd seen my first football match, and might be inclined to watch another, now I understood how the game worked and how much it meant to the fans in the stadium. Then in the pub I'd had a rare conversation with other adults who weren't schoolteachers. I may not have fully convinced them this time, but my sharp intellect would surely prevail if given another shot. Finally, at the party, I'd encountered other guests who obviously found me attractive, and next time our *rendezvous sentimental* might last longer and be more fulfilling. And if I were to tell the tale again, then the off-the-cuff witty remark which I'd been saving up for years would surely receive the applause that it truly deserved.

At least as good as *Carry On Matron*, then, and far better than marking a pile of schoolbooks.

FROM TRUMPER WITH LOVE

Editor's note: This is the only piece of Peter Trumper's writing to be set entirely in the third person. It's clear that Trumper is the author: his prose, particularly when he attempts to write French, is quite individual. This story might mark a point when he considered publishing his tales, and he felt a third person narrative was more bookish. Or maybe it is less truthful than its predecessors, and Peter felt the creation of a fictional alter ego was called for. Perhaps he was aiming for the style and aura of Ian Fleming's James Bond. Fleming, as readers may know, consistently refers to his hero by surname alone, and liked to think of his own service in Naval Intelligence as the inspiration for his hero's exploits.

Sadly, we can only speculate.

Sebastian Bryant

Peter Trumper was quite the ladies' man. The hunter, or *la chaussure*, as the French put it. They also say *le courrier de jupes,* the man who chases after skirts.

As a schoolmaster, he considered parents' evenings a rich hunting ground. He was often attracted to single mothers of around his age, which, as he often reminded people, was 32.

That sometimes led to embarrassment: some mothers who attended alone were in fact married, their husband having stayed at home to look after younger children. They, naturally, resisted Trumper's charms. Sometimes, he was drawn towards women who had taken trouble over their appearance for parents' evening, applying make-up and wearing their smartest clothes, but then he remembered their offspring, slovenly, semi-feral brats with appalling personal hygiene and enough vulgarity to audition for *Love Island*. That made him wonder what the mother was really like when she wasn't making such an effort.

He sometimes discussed matters of the heart with his colleague 'Luvvie' Laithwaite, the head of Drama. Luvvie wasn't interested in the mothers, of course, but single fathers tend not to come to parents' evenings. He often commented, "I notice you're predating the young mothers again tonight, Peter." As always, Trumper had a witty riposte: "I certainly do not pre-date them, Mr Laithwaite. They're my age and more besides."

Two things caused Trumper to step up his search for a partner. First, a rumour at school that he and Luvvie shared the same 'orientation.' Untrue, of course, but the pair had been spotted dining together at the Golden Poppadom, a local Indian restaurant, and people will talk, Trumper reflected. Second, his need for more assistance around the home. His cleaner, Mrs Lee, came in twice a week and kept the house spotless, as well as washing, ironing and making a supply of delicious meals for his fridge and freezer. Trumper was far from useless in the kitchen – he could make a pot of tea and buttered toast – but he cherished the idea of having more constant support. A slice of cake with his tea, for example, or a clean shirt for an unexpected occasion, services which Mrs Lee could provide only on Tuesdays and Saturdays.

It was from Luvvie Laithwaite – ever the gossip – that Trumper learnt something which he quickly saw could be to his advantage. Mr Bryant, the headmaster, had recently split up from his very attractive second wife and moved into a bachelor flat near the school. The children from his first marriage had grown up and left home; the newly separated wife, who was childless, was around ten years younger than the first, so around Trumper's true age. Unattached, good-looking, and wealthy, then. Well worth looking into.

Trumper quickly found Bryant's address from the school office. That Saturday morning, he drove there but deliberately parked two streets away. His brand new Catalunya Red Audi cabriolet would only draw attention if spotted too close to the scene.

James Bond's car, he recalled, had rotating numberplates, a perfect way of avoiding detection, but Trumper had not thought to specify those accessories from the dealership. It made him wonder, through — if Bond had a choice of 4 registration numbers on his Aston Martin, did that mean he had to register the car 4 times ………. and pay 4 times the road tax?

A bus shelter just opposite gave a good view of the Bryant home, and Trumper took up position there. As a handsome man of standout appearance, often compared to a much younger version of the actor Hugh Grant, he appreciated the need for a disguise. It was a damp autumn day, so an overcoat with upturned collar would not look out of place. He also wore dark glasses and a hat — Trumper wasn't a regular hat wearer, but on his last visit, his father had left behind a trilby which Trumper was now happy to borrow. He'd sneaked into Luvvie's drama cupboard on Friday afternoon and borrowed a clip-on beard, but it itched, and the clips tugged at his ears, so he dumped it in the litter bin by the bus stop.

It was a leafy avenue, not the kind where long queues gather to wait for buses, and despite every confidence in his disguise, Trumper was pleased to be alone. Shortly, a woman came out of Bryant's house, locked the front door, and placed the key under a flowerpot on a ground floor windowsill. Not very security-conscious, Trumper thought! She was tall and slim, with blonde shoulder-length hair, a knee-length raincoat and a scarf which covered some of her features. She climbed into a small car – a budget Ford or Vauxhall – and drove away.

The temptation to look inside was too great! Trumper nonchalantly crossed the road, walked calmly up the drive and surreptitiously took the key from where she'd left it. Having taken the car, she was obviously going to be away for some time. No alarm sounded when he let himself in. He dropped his hat and dark glasses on a table in the hallway, next to a vase of cut flowers. The house was tastefully decorated, he noted, as he expertly sized up the abstract paintings on the walls. In the tidy, well-stocked kitchen he found a tin containing some expensive looking biscuits, and he helped himself to a couple. He would return for a few more before leaving! From the hall, a flight of stairs led to a broad landing, where it turned before heading further upwards. Trumper had just reached the first floor when a noise from below stopped him in his tracks. Someone else had entered by the front door, which he had carelessly left unlocked.

The top of the stairs offered no view of the front door and hallway, as it was directly above them. But the intruder had no idea of Trumper's presence, so the advantage of surprise lay with him, if only he chose the moment to use it.

Or had someone been following him and watched him come in? Did Mrs Bryant already have a lover, and might he react violently to discovering he now had a rival?

Trumper could hear the intruder pacing the hallway, then starting to climb the stairs. Edging further along the upstairs corridor, he caught a glimpse of his stalker, who fortunately was looking down at the vacuum cleaner which she – it was a woman, he now realised – was dragging up the stairs. He was startled to recognise her as Mrs Lee, his charlady. Why wasn't she at his house? Saturday mornings were when she was supposed to be doing his cleaning!

He ducked inside the first available door. It led to a bedroom – a spare bedroom, Trumper surmised, as there were no signs of regular use: nothing left lying about, no clothes or dressing gowns hanging casually on the back of the door. No ensuite bathroom either, which a master bedroom would surely have had. The window looked out onto a back garden, and a built-in wardrobe ran the full length of one wall – Trumper was eying up his options for either hiding or escape, should Mrs Lee and her Hoover attempt to enter.

Enter she did! Trumper slipped into the wardrobe and crouched in the dark amongst Mrs Bryant's coats and dresses. Fortunately, the charlady didn't open the sliding doors, and after a few minutes' dusting and vacuuming she moved further along the landing and into the other bedrooms.

No sooner had she left when Trumper's phone pinged. Had she been in the room at the time, she might not have heard it above the vacuum cleaner, but it could easily have given away his hiding place. Carefully exiting the wardrobe, he opened the phone.

The ping was a text message from her, sent about an hour ago, stating that she had another appointment and would come and 'do' him this afternoon, rather than in the morning as was her usual arrangement. Annoyed to see someone else given priority, Trumper forced himself to stay calm as he revised his plan: he'd wait until she was gone before making his escape.

His inspection of the wardrobe's contents confirmed what he'd spotted earlier. Mrs Bryant was indeed slim and of above average height. Her clothes were a mix of high street brands and designer labels. Nothing vulgar or tarty, he noted, apart from something which struck him as soon as he saw it. No fewer than three nurses' uniforms hung among the other items. Trumper had read about couples who enjoy dressing up to please one another in games of a sexual nature, and it amused him to think that Mrs Bryant used to do that for the cold fish that he'd always assumed the headmaster to be. This cast their relationship in a different light, and he wondered how he might tell Bryant that he knew all about his fantasies without revealing how he'd come by the information. Not that he wanted to be critical; a woman in a nurse's outfit can be extremely attractive, as Trumper knew from watching his much-loved collection of *Carry On* films, in which celebrated actresses such as Barbara Windsor, Hattie Jacques and various others play nurses to great effect.

His plans to leave the house as he'd entered were rapidly undone. He heard Mrs Lee put the Hoover away, then take out an ironing board which she set up on the landing. Where to hide now? If she put the ironing away, it would surely be in the wardrobe, where he'd be discovered immediately if he hid there again. Instead, he crouched behind the door, hoping that if she did come in, he'd be out of her line of sight. Eventually, he heard her putting the ironing board away, and assumed she was getting ready to leave. But then came the sound of the front door being opened again, and an exchange of voices.

"All in order, Mrs B," Mrs Lee was saying. "I'll be on my way, then."

"So glad you could come at short notice," the other voice replied, which he took to be that of Mrs

Bryant. "I've got you-know-who coming this afternoon, so thanks again for rearranging. Back to normal next week, alright?"

It was clear that as Mrs Lee left, Mrs Bryant would be staying. The window now became his only means of escape. A return to the biscuit tin in the kitchen was out of the question. From the first floor window ledge, the drop was about ten feet. Fortunately, a garden wall halved the distance, if he could be sure of alighting on it. He opened the window and climbed through. If Mrs Bryant came in after he'd gone, she'd assume Mrs Lee had opened it to air the room.

He suddenly remembered he'd placed his hat on the table downstairs, with the sunglasses inside it. No chance of going back for them now! They'd be noticed, he realised, but short of fingerprinting, nothing could link them to him. Summoning up his courage, he dropped from the window ledge, aiming to plant both feet onto the wall. But the capping stone was damp, and his foot slipped from under him, throwing him off balance. He toppled further and crashed to the ground. Pain shot up his leg, and as he fell, the brickwork tore and drew blood from his hand and wrist. Badly shaken, he could see that he'd fallen into a passageway between Bryant's garden and its neighbour. He limped under cover of the wall on one side and a tall wooden fence on the other into a back street, and from there he was able to hobble back to his car.

He managed to drive home, despite a throbbing down one side and no feeling in his ankle. Too faint to eat, he couldn't face Mrs Lee when she came to do his cleaning in the afternoon, so he made a cup of sweet tea and went straight to bed, leaving her a note to say he had the flu and was not to be disturbed. On Sunday, his foot was giving him even more pain, but by supporting it on a pile of cushions and taking regular doses of paracetamol, he was able to concentrate enough to glance through his lessons for the following week and keep up with the day's news on his phone. By early evening he felt shattered, so he poured himself a large glass of whisky and went to bed. Once the whisky had numbed the pain, he slept like a log.

On Monday morning he was still suffering and his ankle had swollen to the size of a football. He couldn't possibly drive to school – or stand in front of his pupils – so he phoned the school office and said he'd broken his foot and was going to A&E. How would he get there, they asked? He said he'd phone for an ambulance, but they said no, they'd find a colleague who wasn't teaching first lesson and could come out and drive him. Ten minutes later John Crick, the Maths teacher, turned up at his door. At the hospital, Crick helped him into the waiting room, but as soon as the two men had spoken to the receptionist and Trumper had taken a seat, he left as he needed to get back to his classes.

"As soon as they let you out," Crick had said, "for goodness' sake don't wait for an ambulance. Just call school – somebody'll come and take you home. If it's after school, here's my number – ring me." And off he went.

Trumper waited for what seemed an eternity, and wished he'd taken more of the paracetamol, or perhaps another dose of the whisky, before leaving home. The receptionist wouldn't help – she wasn't allowed to dispense any palliative at all, but that gave Trumper an opportunity he had been waiting for.

"In that case, I'll have a large vodka martini, shaken but not stirred!" he quipped.

Unimpressed, the receptionist rolled her eyes and told him to return to his chair at once.

"Ooh, Matron!" he replied, in his best Kenneth Williams voice, and she glared at him in a manner he found most arousing.

By eleven o'clock, Trumper was starting to feel peckish. He'd had no breakfast and now was just the time he'd be heading to the school canteen for a cup of coffee and a cream doughnut. A new receptionist – a great hippopotamus of a woman – had come on duty since his arrival, so he asked her whether there was somewhere he could buy a cake or sandwich without forfeiting his place in the queue.

"And what exactly is wrong with you?" she demanded.

"Isn't it obvious? I'm hungry!" he replied.

"I mean what's wrong with you medically?" she insisted.

"That's a good question. If I ever get to see a doctor, I'm sure he'll know at once."

She looked at him harshly, and he relented. "I think I've broken my ankle," he said.

In that case, she decreed, no food was permitted in case he needed an anaesthetic.

"I'd rather have an anaesthetic than have to look at you, fatso," he muttered under his breath. He knew the real reason she didn't want him to have anything to eat. Whatever he bought from the canteen would mean less for her!

Finally, his turn came around. A Black African lady emerged from a side door and called out, "Meester Trompeur! Will you please to follow me zis way?"

Trumper tried to stand up, but the pain prevented him. The nurse called for a wheelchair and a porter soon arrived to whisk him down the corridor.

"*Vous avez un accent comique,*" he observed, "*Vous êtes Français, n'est-ce pas?*" Of course, he knew she wasn't – the sunshine in France wouldn't be strong enough to give its citizens a complexion like hers!

"I come from ze Congo," she replied. "French is our official language."

"*Je suis professeur de français,*" he told her. "*Je parle très très bien, n'est-ce pas?*"

"I'm going to take you for an x-ray," she explained. "We need to see if your ankle is broken. Zen we can find ze best course of treatment."

"*Vous ne parlez pas à moi en français. Pourquoi pas?*" he demanded.

"*Bon Dieu, c'est bien évident, n'est-ce pas,*" was what she appeared to say.

After being x-rayed, Trumper was wheeled back to the reception area. A further long wait ensued, during which he became hungrier and hungrier. His frustration mounted as he watched the other A&E patients – a sad bunch of malingerers in his view – being ushered through to treatment and no doubt release. He wished he'd brought something to read, a magazine or even a book to hold up and proclaim himself a person of intellect and refinement.

Finally, the receptionist approached. It was yet another receptionist by now – the first two must have finished their shifts and gone home. "Mister Trumper, will you go through to physiotherapy?" she asked.

The word startled him. He imagined a swarthy, musclebound torturer grinning hysterically, pummelling his fleshy areas and twisting his joints until they cracked from the pain. But jumping to his feet and running away was beyond him, and he surrendered to being manhandled back into the wheelchair and trundled along another corridor. Through the frosted glass of a consulting room door, he could make out a figure sitting on a swivel chair. He imagined his adversary stroking a fluffy white cat as it purred on his lap.

Opening the door revealed a different picture. No cat, but a tall, slim lady in a nurse's uniform sitting on the chair. Her badge read, 'Brenda Bryant, Chief Physiotherapist.' Trumper suddenly rediscovered the ability to stand up. Clamping her hand in his, he introduced himself: "The name's Trumper, Peter Trumper. *Enchanté, madame.*"

"Mr Trumper," she said sweetly, as she withdrew her hand, "Let's see what we can do for you."

Suddenly, everything fell into place. The physiotherapist was Mr Bryant's former wife. The nurse's uniforms in her wardrobe weren't part of a weird mating ritual with her ex-husband, but her daily working clothes. How lucky that Trumper hadn't told anyone about his previous assumptions!

He studied her carefully. An elegant woman indeed, and a professional too! Her initials made him think of another BB, Brigitte Bardot. Once he got to know her better, he might tease her about being his second choice of 'BB.' But if their relationship developed and she was lucky enough to become the first Mrs Trumper, then 'BB' would be meaningless.

"A few details, please, Mr Trumper," she asked. "Your profession?"

"I'm Head of Department at the town's most prestigious high school," he proudly told her. But he knew that when chatting up a woman, it's important to ask questions too, so he added, "And yours?"

"Intergalactic explorer," she said, drily.

"Really? That sounds terribly exciting. I've often thought about becoming an astronaut myself. I'd be very good at it – 'Houston we have lift off! All systems go!'"

"Mr Trumper," she replied, flatly, "this is the physiotherapy department. I'm wearing a physio's overall. You've come to me with a sprained ankle."

Trumper realised this wasn't a good start. She possibly expected him to laugh at her little joke, rather than fall for it, and his courage in the face of suffering didn't seem to impress her either, since she dismissed it as a mere 'sprained ankle.'

"So, for your profession, I'll put schoolteacher," she concluded. "I've looked at your x-rays, and I can see your ankle isn't broken. You've twisted some muscles, though. Can you tell me how it happened?"

Of course, Trumper wasn't going to tell her that he'd injured his ankle trying to escape from her bedroom, so he improvised. "I was at home," he said. "I tripped over something my stupid cleaner had carelessly left at the top of the stairs, then I tumbled all the way down and ended up on my ankle."

By shifting the blame onto his cleaner, Trumper hoped he could persuade Mrs Bryant that he needed more attention than Mrs Lee was able to give him. Mrs Bryant would never do anything like leaving a bulky item on the stairs!

"There's also severe grazing to your hand and wrist," she continued. "Are your stairs made out of rough bricks?"

"Oh no," he reassured her, "the grazing comes from a different mishap. I fell when I was getting out of my car. I mistook the distance – it's a very large car, a bright red top-of the range Audi convertible, with –"

"You need to put plenty of antiseptic on that," she interrupted. Trumper felt deflated; women were supposed to be in awe of a man who could talk about his luxury motor, but she didn't seem thrilled. A pity – he'd bought it and chosen the colour with romantic conquests in mind.

"As for your ankle, you need to rest, but also do some light exercise," she advised. "Can you lie on the couch, please?"

This was more promising! He imagined her saying that to him later in their relationship, and the sexual acrobatics it might lead to. For the moment, though, he simply did as she asked. She made him stretch and rotate his ankle, explaining that he needed to do that repeatedly, stopping before it became painful, until he could comfortably put weight on it and walk normally.

"How long can I expect to stay off school?" he asked.

"A couple of days," she suggested. "After that, it should feel easier. Are you a games man?"

"Oh yes," he said at once, knowing how women admire a man who is sporty and athletic, "I play football. I was the man of the match in the staff versus pupils game."

"Good," she said. "It may take a little longer before you're ready for the rough and tumble, but keep doing what I've shown you, and you'll soon be fine."

"Thank you, Nurse," he said, realising at once that 'nurse' was probably the wrong thing to call her. 'Mrs Bryant' sounded wrong too; nor were they on 'Brenda' and 'Peter' terms just yet. "How quickly should I see you again?"

"If you don't feel better in the next few days," she said, "then you could come again with a GP referral. But I expect you'll notice a difference pretty soon."

Trumper's recovery was a little slower than she'd predicted, and he took a full week off school, but he was walking normally well before the weekend. He knew he hadn't made the most of his first meeting with Brenda; he'd mentioned his status, his car and his sporting prowess, but had failed to tell her about his scholarly talents. His superb French drew many compliments, and he spoke several other European languages too; he recalled the staff at *La Dolce Vita* assuming he was Italian as he ordered so fluently when dining there with George Roland, the Ofsted inspector. How could he make her aware of his accomplishments in that field too?

Suddenly – but too late – it occurred to Trumper that Brenda might have been trying to give him encouraging signals all the time. By asking if he was a 'games man,' perhaps she didn't mean the football field but something more intimate. Saying he'd soon be ready for the 'rough and tumble' could be taken the same way. And when she told him he could 'come again soon,' how he wished he'd answered, "As the actress said to the bishop" – a classic line from one of his favourite *Carry On* films.

Undaunted, Trumper hit upon a plan. He would invite Brenda to dinner at his house, a meal to be cooked and served by his charlady, Mrs Lee. He selected the date: the following Friday. He could leave Mrs Lee to clean and cook before he got back from a late meeting at school. He'd return home around 8:00, and he'd invite Brenda to arrive at the same time. He had full confidence in Mrs Lee's excellent cooking, and he'd buy the most expensive bottle of French wine that Waitrose could sell him.

He delivered the invitation to the hospital by hand, asking the receptionist to make sure it was passed on immediately to Mrs Bryant. He even used one of his special cards – he had a stock of them, a photograph of himself on the front, with space for a message inside, and he wrote:

My dearest Brenda, please accept my grateful thanks for treating me so wonderfully during my physiotherapy visit last Monday. I am delighted to say that thanks to your tender care I have made a complete recovery. I would like to invite you to a *soirée* which will commence *chez moi* at 8.00 p.m. this Friday. My staff will be serving a *diner gastronomique* and my extensive wine cellar will be open! RSVP, Peter

He felt there was enough French in there to make his mastery of the language apparent, and the photograph was particularly good, taken a few years ago at a professional studio. It was a smaller copy of the framed one which hung in his hallway. Of course, he added his address and phone number.

Then he instructed Mrs Lee to swap her usual Saturday duties for Friday and asked her what she thought she should buy and prepare. He also told her to turn up wearing something appropriate for serving a meal – he didn't want her looking like a cleaner, or worse still, like a school dinner lady. It remained only to await Brenda's reply.

As Friday evening approached, he had heard nothing from her. He was just about to set off for the meeting at school when there was a knock at his door. Not Brenda arriving early, but Lizzy Lee, his cleaner's daughter who also happened to be a pupil in his sixth form class, alongside a scruffy young man he took to be her boyfriend. Trumper was annoyed – Mrs Lee had no business telling her daughter where he lived. Moreover, if the girl wanted remedial assistance beyond the outstanding teaching which he already provided, then she should ask for it in school time. It transpired she only wanted to tap her mother up for a few pounds to go out on the town, but Trumper sent her away with a flea in her ear. He didn't hold with the opinion that the girl was talented and should apply to Oxford; she asked questions in class which undermined his authority, and her work lacked the deference which he expected from his pupils. Mr Bryant took her side, but Trumper suspected that if she ever got to Oxford, she would probably ask around after him and discover that he wasn't really an *omnibus*, as he knew former Oxford students were called.

No reply from Brenda, then. Trumper returned from school to find that Mrs Lee had everything else in hand. She suggested looking in the 'spam' folder of his incoming messages – a horrific idea! Trumper would gladly look under 'ribeye steak' or *'filet mignon,'* but never in anything so vulgar as 'spam,' 'corned beef,' or 'meat hash.' Mrs Lee showed him how, and there it was: Brenda's reply, which had been sent the very day he dropped off his card:

Dear Peter, Thank you for your kind invitation. I'm sorry I can't make your party on Friday. This week I'm on late shift and don't finish until 10:00 pm. I hope your *soirée* goes well and you and all your other guests have a wonderful time. Glad to hear you're much better. Brenda Bryant B Sc (Hons) Chief Physiotherapist

A corporate reply. From her NHS address. A definite lack of intimacy there! But Trumper thought quickly, as he so often did. He told Mrs Lee there was no response from his companion, so he was still expecting her at any moment. In the meantime, she could start to serve him his dinner. If by the end of the evening there was still no sign of her, then she was under no circumstances to pass that information on to her daughter. The story was to be that his partner had arrived, the meal was a total success, and her catering services had ended at the point when it might be assumed that he and his date would retire to bed together.

Over the weekend, Trumper wondered whether Brenda deserved a second chance. He didn't want to appear short of options; as he often told the office ladies at school, when they tried to fix him up on a date with one of the younger teachers, "I may be single, but I'm certainly not desperate!"

Trumper knew full well that, as the French say, "*Il y a autre poisson dans la mer.*" Well, he would catch some of those other fish! If he was the hunter, *la chaussure,* then he could also be the fisherman, *le poissonnier.* Even as he thought it, his rod was starting to quiver, as the bishop said to the actress.

Yes, Trumper would definitely be back.

ABOUT THE AUTHOR

Stephen Hudson is from Yorkshire.   He's a translator and interpreter in the legal, commercial and medical sectors and has taught French and German to A-Level students.   He is also the author of the teen fiction 'Mister French' (Austin Macauley, 2023) and the thriller 'The Body in the Graveyard' (Austin Macauley, 2024).